The London Silence

Stephen Moran was born in Dublin and steeped in the humours that billow in nightly from the sea to pervade that black city. He now lives and works in London where he finds most of his inspiration, and more than enough wonder.

This story collection carries us like an outgoing tide, on a wave retreating from the underworld of 21st century London to a Dublin hinterland in the 70's, 60's and beyond, to the time of coalmen, tenements, and bicycles.

I0554454

THE LONDON SILENCE

STEPHEN MORAN

Pretend Genius Press

www.pretendgenius.com

First edition 2004
Second edition 2020

Published simultaneously in the UK and the US
by Pretend Genius Press

'Kenny' was first published in *Bird Times*
'Wanker' was first published in *Write This*

ISBN 0-9747261-4-1

*This book is a work of fiction and the characters and events in it exist
only in its pages and in the author's imagination.*

For
Molly & Christy

Contents

I: Around the Dear Ruin

II: All Those Endearing Young Charms

I

Around the Dear Ruin

The London Silence

"A Tube train with more than 100 terrified passengers on board rolled backwards in a tunnel for over half a mile after the driver apparently fell asleep at the controls. The Northern line train went backwards through Chalk Farm station, gathering speed all the time." (July 11th. 2000)

Murphy got on the Jubilee underground line at Green Park after attending a literary launch at a club in St James. He'd taken a little too much free chardonnay, much too quickly, one of the occupational hazards of being a critic. He was racked with self-consciousness when he boarded, as he always was on public transport, but he was just starting to relax in the afterglow of the wine as the train reached Baker Street.

The scrolling display opposite said 'The next station is St John's Wood.' He remembered hearing something about the tunnel having to be diverted to avoid a plague burial pit on the long haul between Baker Street and St

John's Wood. Such a long interval, it felt as if the train had got lost in the night, and it crossed his mind that they had crashed and were really all dead, that the next station would be in the afterlife.

The train's initial noise like wind howling, turned to a rhythmic hammering. After that it started to sound like a slowed down recording of somebody saying something. Murphy looked rightwards to the far end, through the windows of the connecting doors, where the yellow-lit following carriage switched angles, following the inclines and bends of the track.

Everyone was sitting quietly. For a change there were no builders swearing, no Balkan beggars with babies under shawls, going from carriage to carriage, no cackling teenage girls. A young man in dusty clothes had fallen asleep and slumped sideways. A homely old couple were talking but Murphy couldn't hear what they were saying above the racket of the train pouring in through the vents on top of the dirty windows.

It was comforting to think that he had just been to a fancy party in St. James. That was something to give one confidence, an answer to any ill-concealed contemptuous glance. The other passengers had all been working late in rat-holes of offices, he presumed, while he had been consorting with middle-ranking celebrities and pocket geniuses. Not to mention the odd gazelle.

A young woman with a short skirt was sitting a few seats away. It was summer above them. Beside him was somebody in jeans, with their legs apart. He assumed it was a young man. The less self-aware a young man is, he thought, the wider apart he spreads his legs when he sits. It is a territorial claim, an aggression, like spitting in the street. But when he looked around, he saw that it was not a man but a woman. She had brown hair and wore a small denim jacket over a camisole.

Her right arm and shoulder had been touching Murphy's left, and her foot tapped against his, making him move his leg slightly. This was not good. You had to sit perfectly still; he had learned that much by observing how people sat who were calm. It was very difficult to keep still while nervous, worse than allowing Saint Vitus's dance to take over, but one had to try and keep up appearances.

Still the train trundled and the fluorescent tubes glared. Murphy was sitting bent to his right by now to avoid the person next to him. The rocking of the train made their shoulders touch again. He longed for the time before he looked around and saw that she was what he would call a girl, a young woman really. Murphy had been thinking of himself as a sort of wise guru, distant from the distractions around him. Now he had changed and started reminding himself that he was sure to be the first one to panic if anything went wrong, and that disasters were always happening.

He squirmed heavily in his seat. The doors of the carriage flapped and rattled as the train clanked on. The blurred candy and dirt coloured wires along the sides of the tunnel traced a wavy line behind the scratchy glass between the tube train and the tight black tunnel. Still the electronic display scrolled, 'The next station is St. John's Wood.'

The lights went off and the electric motors whirred quickly down to silence. There was absolute dark for a few seconds then a couple of dim single bulbs came on near the doors in the middle of the carriage. The fluorescent tubes stayed off. 'Great,' he said, aloud. That word must have told everyone in the carriage that yes, Murphy would be the first to panic.

There was a London silence, the only thing that enabled most people to get to and from work in peace, which could last for an age. Londoners could sit there forever, ignoring other people. They assumed the train would move soon and the white noise walls would spring up again between everyone. Eventually though, ignoring other people would become untenable and they would have to talk.

Murphy's unguarded word was the first crack. Coming so soon, it marked him as an outsider, a foreigner, someone who didn't know how things were done. They would have detected his vestigial Irish accent. He didn't care, he hated people who wouldn't say anything, people who wouldn't tell you what you needed to know, the kind of people who wouldn't give you the steam off their piss. He wished his accent had not been bastardised after twenty-five years away from home, or else that it had completely vanished.

The old couple were silent now, holding hands, down the other end of the carriage. The old man had a white moustache and was nearly bald. The corner of his mouth indicated that he was displeased but not surprised by the breakdown. The woman with him was wearing a red woollen coat. She looked confused.

Two lanky young men in suits, sprawling on seats near the doors, started to talk. It was so quiet that it was as if they were talking to everyone. 'I said that Nigel was going to...' 'Damn! You know then, pretty well...' 'Yah, look, I said you've gotta trim.' 'Right.' 'Exactly, what else could you say?' 'Yah.'

Murphy noticed how one of a pair on public transport always talks and talks, while the other 'mmms,' 'yeses' and 'nos.' You wonder what the quiet one is thinking. It would be more interesting to hear about that. Mostly they're just embarrassed to be with Big Mouth.

Surely the train would move soon. The emergency bulbs were flickering. The destination display scroller was dead. The driver could at least have made an announcement. The girl beside Murphy had shifted and leaned away from him. 'Bloody marvellous, isn't it?' he said. After a moment, she got up to change places. So timid. That's another thing he hated. Just as she moved, the fluorescent lights came back on, the electric motors started revving up, and the electronic display started scrolling again.

The train started to move forward and the girl sat

down directly opposite him. Shit. Now he had nowhere to look. The scrolling display offered another phrase, 'Change here for the Metropolitan Line.' How little of interest there was, what a waste of time. He directed his gaze to the printed advert slotted in its frame above her, the nuisance. It said, 'Are you sitting opposite the new man in your life? Call Datelink.'

Murphy's reflection was spread over the curve of the half-lit glass behind her. In it he saw himself as a fatheaded monster. The other people seen through his peripheral vision were revealed as zombies. They had faces like cabbage patch dolls with coaly black smudges instead of eyes and mouths. Often one of them would have her mouth wide open, permanently yawning, as if she had a toothpick stuck between her lips, gaping helplessly like beached fish.

When Murphy looked around, the old man with the white moustache was smiling an 'I knew it' smile. There was still no announcement from the driver, and the train continued to move much more slowly than usual. The electronic display was now scrolling the message 'This train terminates here. Please take your belongings with you.'

The train stopped with a jolt and blacked out completely. The girl in the short skirt, it must have been, let out a small scream. 'Oh here we go again,' one of the young men in suits was heard saying.

'Fucking hell,' the other one said.

It was dizzyingly dark, there was nothing by which to

orient oneself. The emergency lights didn't come on this time. Murphy felt more than nervous; he felt fear, thinking about another train crashing into theirs, leaving them pinned in the dark to die slowly, painfully from their crush injuries, and suffocating in smoke.

Somewhere above them, people were doing all the things that people do on top of the thin concrete shell. The plague dead marbled the earth in between. Far below, molten magma was looking for a pressure valve, somewhere to blast out. Trains were speeding in all directions and one of them might be on a collision course.

Somebody touched his knee. 'Huh,' he blurted. The person felt along to find the seat beside Murphy and sat down there, clutching his arm. It must've been the girl in the jeans who'd been sitting opposite, but in the absolute darkness he just couldn't tell. Why didn't she say something? She must be mute. Was it even her? It could be anyone. 'Hello,' he said. He felt stupid when there was no answer.

One of the young men down near the doors flicked a cigarette lighter on for a few seconds. His face materialised like a Rembrandt portrait in the dense blackness, simpering, then disappeared again.

From Murphy's left came a metallic clanking sound of the doors to the next carriage forward being opened. A man's voice said, 'Are you all okay in here?'

The girl in the miniskirt started whimpering. The old lady shouted, 'No we're bloody not okay!' and the old

13

man chimed in with, 'What's happening!'

Murphy asked the unseen one, 'Are you the driver?'

Just then the train started to move, trundling. The lights were still off and there was no sound from the electric motors. In the darkness, it was impossible to tell whether they were moving backwards or forwards.

'It's rolling downhill,' said the voice. 'Shit!'

By the sound of the inter-carriage doors clanking and slamming again, whoever it was had gone as near to running as he could manage in the pitch blackness, back towards the front of the train.

The swaying and bouncing of the carriage increased. Murphy still couldn't tell if they were going forwards or backwards. Backwards would be worse. Whoever it was beside him clutched tighter to his left arm. The girl in the miniskirt started to scream repeatedly, short screams. The youths were uttering swear words as if they were prayers.

He hadn't been the first to panic after all.

The Get-Well Card

Christopher's widow, Colleen, sat in the front pew all in black and her hair was black too. Inconsolable, she had been crying for two days and nights. A folk group lilted As Gentle as Silence while we queued in the aisle to pass by his coffin and place our *In Memoriam* cards on a tray.

Her children, older today but still children, held in their emotions. Colleen accepted some brief, futile words from the guests as they filed past on their way to their places. When it came to my turn she stood up, and we talked with hands held.

'Oh Joseph, thanks very much for coming!' she said. 'That card you sent meant so much to Chris. He laughed when he read it, for the first time in months. And his face lit up, he was like the old Christopher.'

The church was full to overflowing. He had been dying for three years. The priest read out a poem that Christopher himself had written for the occasion. The poem was to tell his family he would still be with them, and they would all be together again. It said, 'do not think that you have lost my love/for I am waiting up above…'

After the service the stone-walled church car park was crowded. The hearse was waiting in the tree-dappled, early autumn light. Christopher's mother, in her seventies, wore a look of mild contentment; it had been a blessed release. She was homely, and comfortable in her weight. Thoughtlessly I asked, 'How are you keeping?' as she waited for the first black limousine to pull up.

'I'm not too bad,' she said. 'In the circumstances.'

I was only an exile over from London after so many years out of touch. I had been to the house the night before, with some of my family. We parked in the street and joined the series of friends and neighbours who came and went through the open front door. The local stream and fields nearby made the evenings damp now that summer had passed its height. It was the hour when lights start to come on before the sun sets. I had never seen a dead body before, and was determined not to this time.

Everyone was calmer than I had expected. His sister, now the eldest, hugged me and said my name. She looked shocked. A miniature of her mother with the same red hair. They had lost the main man of their family for the second time. Her father had died some years before. She said Colleen was being comforted in another room.

'Joseph! His childhood pal,' Aunt June said to me when I made my way through to the kitchen. She was sitting on a chair in the middle of the floor, accepting condolences with equanimity from all who appeared.

'It was a blessed release,' I said.

'It was,' she said. 'Thank God he's suffering no more. It was dreadful, Joseph. Have you seen him?'

'No, not yet.'

'Go on up, now, and say goodbye to him, Joseph.'

My resistance fell. There was no room for argument with her mild exhortation.

Upstairs people came one at a time, some lingering a while, or kneeling by the bed while others passed through. Something peaceful was there in the room. The curtains were closed, yet the evening light came through them and filled the place with grey air. In the middle of the big bed he lay. On top of the coverlet his hands twined a set of rosary beads. The cancer had reduced him from a middleweight to a featherweight. Completely bald and with alien narrowness, he looked like a waxwork of an old man in peaceful sleep. We were about the same age, early forties. I touched his hand in farewell, and I hoped that death was not contagious.

We used to call him Christy but in his adopted town they knew him as Kit. He had coached the youth football team for several years, and led the Scouts every week too, even after it was known that he had a terminal illness. His faithful circle of friends in the local pub at the bottom of the hill, kept him a place at the bar. The local newspaper printed his story on the day of the funeral; a Dub who had coached the local Gaelic football team, while remaining loyal to the Blues. He had continued his voluntary work through many operations. But most of all he was remembered for his unfailing bonhomie and good cheer.

Later that night the undertakers had to carry him downstairs to put him in his coffin, and we all followed to the church for a short service. Afterwards the cold night fog pierced us to the core as we walked down the hill from the church on our way to the pub. I said, 'I'll be surprised if another five or six people don't get their death out of this'.

An honour guard of scouts in their uniforms formed up beside the hearse with pennants of county and town. Christopher's coffin was draped in the tricolour. Footballers followed next in their team jerseys. The funeral cortege moved out of the churchyard and down the hill towards the centre of town. Scores of people walked behind the hearse, followed by cars with those who were too grief-stricken or not able to walk the two or three miles to the cemetery.

We descended to the main street, where all of the shops were closed out of respect as we passed by. I couldn't help but grieve, in spite of a self-conscious helplessness, a sense of unworthy public display. Soon the cortege would turn and pass by Christopher's house before heading a mile and a half out of town to the cemetery.

One summer our families holidayed together in Arklow, a harbour town on the estuary of the river Avoca in Wicklow. Christopher being a scout, and his younger brother Luke too, led the way on long expeditions. I was a slow-foot.

'We better walk quicker or it will take too long to get there,' Christopher said, 'and then it will be dark coming back.'

We walked upriver from Arklow to Woodenbridge, beyond the copper mines where the tumbling river water changed back from bronze to silver coloured. The last part of the way we trudged along railway tracks under the blazing sun. It was evening when we reached the fishing place, under a bridge where the river was as wide as a small road, and languid. The trout were biting, making many circlets in the water and occasionally jumping into the air and back with a little splash. Only Christopher had a fishing rod, so we just sat and watched him fly fishing.

After looping into the side street and stopping for a minute outside his house, the cortege turned back to the main road. There was no shade now from the afternoon sun. The retinue stretched as we climbed the road out of town. Some chatted in groups as they walked. Outsiders like myself walked alone. We turned a corner after the last houses, onto a wide concrete road flanked on both sides by grass verges and footpaths. There were two schools set far back in their grounds on either side. What a sight to see, lined up beside the daisies and buttercups of the grass verges, all the little children of the schools, boys on one side, girls on the other standing with their hands up in prayer, waiting for us to pass by.

He was always the life and soul of the party. The last time we had met was at a niece's twenty-first birthday party. Christopher was not expected to be able to take up his invitation along with Colleen and the kids, because he had just come out of hospital the previous day. They had cut more of his insides away and there was not much left. The disease was spreading. He was thin and mostly bald, but no less amiable and happy-go-lucky it seemed.

'Still drinking and smoking I see – do they allow that?' I asked as we clinked glasses of stout – mine a half, his a pint.

'Why not? You can't let the bastards get you down!'

That summer in Arklow, the background music everywhere had been School's Out and Layla. The streets were crowded in the daytime, when we went to the outdoor pool and watched the girl in the white swimsuit, transparent when wet, sitting with her feet in the cobalt blue water. I was doing a lot of diving. We pretended to be German tourists and kept up the fake accents for the whole holiday. In all likelihood it was only ourselves we made laugh. We went down by the harbour and tried to con the fishermen unloading trawlers there.

'Ve are from Deutschland,' he told them.

'I am Kurt und zis is Wolfgang,' I said.

'Vos is das?' he said, pointing out a red fish with an ugly, bony head.

They said we could have it, and we brought it back to the house, where Aunt June debated with my mother how to cook it.

We explored the riverside way down along the huge stony, harbour wall. His younger brother Luke walked daredevil on the parapet. I was the only one who worried. We followed round the coast to the cement factory pier where there was a vast white concrete zone with its own cranes and ships. At night the three of us slept in a tent in the back garden of the rented stone house in a tree-lined street south of the town. The clock in a chapel nearby tolled every quarter of an hour for insomniacs. Luke ground his teeth in his sleep, and when he wasn't doing that he was sniffling.

'Have you ever been afraid of nothing?' I asked Christopher before I could sleep one night.

I was shivering and stricken with an abstract wave of fear.

'There's nothing to be afraid of,' he said. 'The house is just there.'

The road narrowed as the procession left the last buildings behind. We came to level ground, surrounded by small pleasant fields with lush vegetation and a few animals, doing nothing but standing in the sun and watching us closely as we passed by.

When we were kids we laughed non-stop, on the few occasions when we met. Our laughter was legendary in the family. Perhaps because we were so different; he was all out and I was all in. Christopher turned into a pubgoer, qualified and got himself the best job he could imagine – out and about in the countryside as a surveyor. He married Colleen and soon they had their first child. I became a loner, living a life of drudgery in a factory by day and doing nobody knew what by night.

Whenever there was a party, he would sing and demand ballads, and I would play my guitar. His party piece was Spancil Hill. *I dreamt I held her in my arms as in the days of yore – She said Johnny you're only joking as many a time before...* Everyone wanted me to be like him. With drink taken we would arrange to meet at the pub, but one of us would always forget and not turn up. He was better at school, at drawing, at work – at everything. The only thing I was better at was singing, and I could accompany myself. I had a dash of flair for performance.

The night of the party, with most of his stomach gone, Christopher got too drunk. It had been a disco party mostly for the young people, including our own kids, dancing oblivious to the world. Some people had already left, when Christopher called for a sing-song. 'C'mon, give us Seven Drunken Nights!'

His wife and children waited, worrying but not wanting to spoil the night for him. He had been quite a catch for her, Colleen always used to think, and she still thought it then. I shouted a bit of the ballad, and he remarked, 'Joseph as usual, doing the good old Ronnie Drew!'

I thought I heard a bitterness in his voice.

'I think it's time to go home,' I said to his wife and children, to say it for them so they could start.

He had already lived for longer than the doctors gave him after they diagnosed cancer. When I went back to London, I heard from time-to-time how badly he was suffering. A year went by and I felt guilty for not visiting or at least writing. Something was unresolved. Word came that he was no longer able to go out. He was just skin and bone and spent most of his time in bed, in terrible pain. Still if anyone visited he made the effort to get dressed and to sit downstairs with them dutifully.

I picked up a get-well card, though I knew it was really a goodbye card. For weeks I hesitated to send it, because of a sense that in some way it would mean giving permission for him to die, and that I had no right to do that, when his family were considered. It was so late in the end, when I sent it, that I wasn't sure if it had reached him before he died. In it I wrote, 'Don't let der schweinhunds grind you down – with all my love, Joseph.'

The ground was level and muddy but the graves were well tended in that neat country cemetery. The priest said prayers as they laid him to rest, under the flags of the colour party. I was not close. The crowd barred my way, those with whom he had made his new life, who called him Kit and not Christy. On this perfect day in the hinterland of our youth, he had achieved so much more than I ever would. I was an outsider, a nobody, who never even knew what a hero my cousin had become.

The Meeting

The phone call came as a shock. He couldn't remember the last time anybody had contacted him. The caller asked for Brother Boniface, which meant the call related to his years teaching. He thought he re-membered the boy who wanted to meet him, Martin Kelly, but he was hoping it might be a different one.

Discretion told him not to invite the boy to the Brothers' retirement home. He arranged to meet in the old coffee shop on Grafton Street, a place he associated with respectability, and the smell of roasting coffee that announced the genteel part of town. That was maybe twenty years ago.

The big machines were still turning and combing the beans in the windows of the coffee shop. The interior was shabbier than he remembered though, the upholstery out-of-shape and sagging. He had imagined waitresses with white sashes tied in bows, serving the coffee and cream cakes. Instead it was self-service and chaotic in a way that made him feel clumsy and too old to be there.

The cashier said something to him that he didn't hear right. People waiting behind him slid their trays up to his, and didn't think to hide the contempt on their lips.

He had a square, flabby face, a blank screen on which you could see anything or nothing. His eyes were like eyes in a mask, looking out from a place of invisibility and coldness. His jowls were sagging, and his hair mostly a memory, but if he looked in the mirror at a certain angle, he could still think of himself as good looking.

He placed his tray on a table beside one of the bench seats along a wall, where he could face the entrance. He sat down and sank too low behind the table. There were young people all around, so full of themselves, it seemed to him, so arrogant and shallow.

He hoped the boy was not going to dredge up all the sunken filth. It should be left to decay and disappear. He sipped the hot, milky coffee and it tasted the same as it had years ago. The blend was distinctive, the desired coffee tang refined perfectly from its bitter source, the swirling sludge at the bottom of the cup. Leave the sludge to settle, he thought.

A tall, ugly young man looked about to take the seat opposite him.

'Sorry, that seat is taken.'

'Brother Boniface? I wouldn't have recognised you if you hadn't spoken. I'd know that voice anywhere. Do you not recognise me?'

The young man pulled out the chair and hung his coat on the back of it. He had rounded shoulders, and a pockmarked face. He spoke with the accent of a semi-skilled worker.

'Martin Kelly.'

'Oh, Martin, sorry. People change so much. So different when... Yes. Of course.'

They shook hands.

'I'll just get a coffee. Can I get you another?'

'No thanks.'

As he watched the young man go to the counter, something, it must have been the back of him, made Boniface remember. His neck and forehead turned damp with twinges of cold sweat. His stomach felt like it did when he was in a car going over a humpbacked bridge.

It was the bridge over the Liffey near Leixlip, when he was taking the boy to Maynooth for the retreat. The boy's family was religious, the kind that would boast of a priest for a son. Auntie so-and-so kissed the Pope's ring. They were well-in with the Brothers.

He had been giving the boy private lessons after school too, at the teacher's desk in a classroom on the second floor, every weekend. He liked to chalk tasks high on the board, so the boy had to tiptoe and write the answers. All the while on the boy's blind side, Boniface would be leaning deep down in the pocket of his clerical cassock, pressing –

'Cream, Brother?'

He hadn't noticed the boy – not a boy anymore, without any semblance of his former appeal – returning.

'There's no need to call me that. To be honest I never liked it. Just call me Bob, that's what everyone calls me.'

'No! Bobby? Go away! Okay, Bobby it is.'

'Bob, yes. It's been ten years since I was headmaster. I retired early.'

'Yes, I heard about that. What have you been doing since? Bob.'

'I've been helping around the Brothers' retirement home. I've hardly been out of it. In fact, this is the first time I've been in town for years. Martin.'

'Go away. Is that a fact? You were a great help to me with the Maths. I was struggling that year, but you got me through with your extra lessons.'

Was it possible the boy had forgotten about the hotel? Memory is like that – it suppresses things, they say. Boniface had got the three-a.m. jones, and tapped on the boy's bedroom door in the guesthouse. As usual. (He had taken several boys over the years.) He would slip into the room and slide into bed beside them. He'd ask them if they knew about the Facts of Life. Are you developed? No? This is what it will be like.

'What do you want? I'm sorry, I mean you asked to meet me, but you didn't say what about. I have lived an exemplary life for the past ten years. Our religion is one that believes in redemption and the sacrament of forgiveness.'

His voice was a little louder than necessary, and the

self-important people at the tables nearby looked over their shoulders at him for a moment. People were quick to judge. He was no worse than they were. Who knew what they went home to, how many affairs, what incest, how they pilfered from their employers, nursed murderous thoughts, or drove their cars viciously, recklessly, beat their wives and children. They were judging him, ignorant of the life of selfless service he lived.

'Yes, I was weak. But I am the man I am now, not the man I was then.'

Martin Kelly – not a boy, the ugly individual in front of him – didn't know what to say to that. One of the self-satisfied cream cake eaters nearby could be heard saying to his companions, 'Am I the bollix that I am now, or the bollix that I was then?'

'Brother, I mean Bob, the thing is – I've had a bit of trouble since I left school. I, eh, got married too young, and then there was an unfortunate incident.'

'Oh dear.'

'Yes, the way it is – see, we're both men of the world. Well you're not of the world, well anyway – whatever – To cut a long story short, I was having an affair. Several affairs, actually. And my missus saw me sitting in a car, and whatever I was doing at the time, with another woman.'

'Go on.'

'Well, she went berserk. She started shouting, and I got angry and I decided I'd drive off and worry about it later. Anyway, doesn't she hold onto the car and fall on the ground – quite a nasty fall – but she's still shouting.'

'At least she was okay.'

'Not exactly. Not after I backed the car over her, a couple of times. That's how I ended up in the Joy.'

The – what was he? – nonentity appeared to have no sense of guilt about what he was saying. He was obviously some sort of sociopath, or psychopath. Maybe that was what he wanted, violent revenge.

'Excuse me, just a minute.'

Boniface got up and went to look for the toilets. The back of his neck was soaked in sweat, and his balance was only just enough to keep him upright. He was trying to think, but the same stupid phrase kept repeating in his mind, 'That's how I ended up in the Joy.' That was it, it was he who would end up in Mountjoy jail next. The boy – the ugly nondescript individual – was trying to frighten him, in so many words.

Perhaps he should just walk out now, not go back, not even discuss anything with the boy. He thought of his magazines. If he were arrested now, he would not have time to destroy them. They would be found and he would be disgraced. He would be like those priests you see on the television being frogmarched into court, with demonstrators shouting invective and waving placards with insults on them.

He went into a stall in the toilets and peed like a woman. He held his head in his hands, and told himself to steady his nerves. There was no point in walking away, it would only be deferring the problem, prolonging the agony.

'I'm sorry,' he said when he returned. 'I'm a little pressed for time. I have things, commitments, so can you tell me why you wanted to meet me?'

'I need a reference,' said Kelly. 'You're the only one from the school that I could find, and you were the Headmaster there for a while.'

Incredible. He had obviously forgotten about that night in the hotel. Or was it possible he didn't care. God forbid, he had turned into the same sort of creature as Boniface himself. It couldn't be contagious, surely. Suppose he had accidentally hit on a child with the tendency, or that all the children he hit on had gone on to be just like him. No, it didn't bear thinking about.

'Is that all? Why didn't you say so? Certainly, I'll give you a reference. As far as I remember you were a fine, intelligent boy.'

'Yeah. Look at me now. I've brought a piece of paper and a pen, so if you could write it now... I really need it for an interview this week.'

So, there was a small element of extortion in the situation after all, Boniface felt. He took the pen and paper and began to write. He hardly had to think about the words, after years of advanced lying, these paltry fibs came easily to him.

'My mother said you had wandering hands,' said Kelly.

The pen slipped from Boniface's hand and escaped his attempt to grasp it on its way to the floor.

''Don't worry, it won't fall any further' – isn't that what you used to say? 'Just leave it.''

Boniface tried to get the pen, but he had to reach down through the small gap left by his corpulent bulk beside the table. The fingertips of his left hand could hardly reach the pen. He stretched, with his head under the table, but only managed to push the pen farther away. He felt Kelly touch his other hand.

'So this is the wandering hand,' Kelly said, tapping the square fingertips. 'Did you ever see that film about Verlaine and Rimbaud?'

Boniface grunted and continued to grope under the table, finally grabbing the pen and surfacing again. Kelly held Boniface's right wrist down on the table with his left hand, and spread the fingers of it with his right hand. 'Rimbaud does this,' he said, and proceeded to feign stabbing the table in between each pair of digits in turn with a spoon. 'Then he speeds up, and up...' He continued to simulate the game. 'Of course it's the thrill of the danger... Sorry, you were writing...'

The spoon clipped the side of one of Boniface's fingers. 'Oops! Sorry.' Kelly let go of Boniface's hand. 'You can kill somebody with a spoon, you know,' he said. 'In a way it's more satisfactory. I think a chopstick would be best. Stabbed to death with a chopstick. It's blunt, you see. In the neck. Like in that film, Murder in the First, did you see that? He kills the guy who betrayed him by stabbing him in the neck with a spoon.'

One of the people along the table looked at Boniface, nodded and said 'All right?' Boniface smiled back feebly.

Boniface tried to resume writing but this time the words came slowly, one every ten seconds, and his mind had to return to first principles to calculate what each next word should be. He struggled to concentrate over his boiling emotions. Where the table had pressed on his left shoulder felt sore, but he knew it wasn't a heart attack yet.

They had stopped that day in the old Ford Anglia, on the way to Maynooth, because he thought he might have a flat tyre. He thought the same thing every time he drove – but it never was flat. When he really got a puncture, he didn't have to stop to look. He stopped to change the wheel. He didn't have to look, he knew. But he didn't know now, what or where he was. He had to look, he had to think whether he was destined for the hell of a wasted life. So he couldn't be doomed. If he had been he would have known. He wouldn't have had to look.

'Yes, wandering hands she said you had, my mother,' Kelly continued. 'When she went to beg for a place in the school for me.'

Boniface wanted to say that the whole religion thing was just an aspiration, a game of snakes and ladders, and that Confession absolved one of guilt. He wanted to explain to the boy why he put his hands on their

33

breasts, the young mothers who came to the school seeking a place for their sons. You had to lay the groundwork to see how far they would go. Start with a shoulder, to the elbow then. Watch the eyes. It was surprising how many of them condescended to let him feel the nothingness of their breasts. He wanted to say that the boy's mother looked him up and down as he did it.

'That is a slanderous thing to say. I'm sure your mother would never say such a thing – never allow such a thing. I thought so, you only wanted to see if you could get something out of me by threatening me with false accusations. It's very clear now. Here, take your reference, and never contact me again. Nobody would ever believe you anyway, a jailbird.'

It felt as if the restaurant had quietened to listen to their conversation. Some people at the nearby seats looked at them openly.

'Yes, she wanted me to be a priest,' Kelly said. 'But I couldn't live up to it, unfortunately. I was a great dis-appointment to her. Well, thank you for the reference, Brother.'

Kelly, horse-faced, round-shouldered, stood up, and drained the dregs from his coffee cup. 'Cheerio,' he said, took his coat from the back of the chair and walked out.

They never let you forget, Boniface thought. He sipped his cold coffee. It had lost its flavour.

Wanker

I

The practice eventually came to dominate Timothy's life. He was ten when he discovered it while sliding to look over the edge of his bed. At first it produced a continuous pleasant tingling followed by a watery precipitation. The sliding technique was the only way that Timothy knew for a long time.

In the beginning there was no object of desire other than the process itself. Soon contemplation of the organ of pleasure progressed to events surrounding it. He would think about the babysitter bathing him, hitching her steamy horn-rimmed glasses. She squirted cold water onto his back from a small plastic bottle, singing *Catch a Perry Como / Wash his face in Omo / Hang him on the line to dry.* Then it was the big towel, over and under, and all around. *When he's stiff and starchy / Call him Liberace.*

'Is it always like that, your little thing?'
'Only sometimes.'

He had to maintain a state of semi-arousal to keep crushing the penis without starting to tear the foreskin, and he found there was most pleasure in a gradually increasing engorgement. If he became too erect, he would put away the memory until he subsided enough to start pressing again.

Soon they would be in sixth class, the last year of Primary, so Brother Francis said it was time for their parents to tell them the Facts of Life. Lying in bed that night, he heard his father coming up the stairs, and called him to tell him what Brother Francis had said. His father sat on the edge of the bed, with just a little light from the doorway coming through. The Facts of Life, well it's the way that men and women make little babies, his father said. You know the thing that you pee-pee with, and girls have a different one, well the boy puts his thing into the girl's and that's how they make a baby. That's about all there was to it.

Timothy wished he could have stayed ten forever, but his days of running in the street would have to end, days of clanging tireless bicycle wheels along with a stick, catching bees, tying knots in the grass to trip up other kids. People would be telling him now that it was no longer sensible to go out in the rain and sail ice pop sticks along new rivers in spate beside the kerb, even in a raincoat and sou'wester; that it was a waste of his time standing in the porch to watch raindrops bouncing off concrete. He would never again be famous in soccer exploits with Latinate writhing on the ground when tripped, imagining agony like a hero tied up and lashed in a Roman epic.

Already the first tiresome school exam was on the horizon. The blonde girl down the street became shrill and scratchy when he touched her accidentally, and she made it clear he was not for her. Even the girl next door moved away when he sat beside her on the back doorstep, and said she didn't want to get pregnant. On a street corner the boys were having discussions about whether oriental women's things were sideways; the place to squeeze a woman to get your way with her – the back of the knees some said – and other tenets of popular biology. They agreed a secret language, in case anyone approached while they talked, in which Cinerama meant sex, and what a girl had between her legs was a plaza. The worst words they knew not to say if adults were around were 'sex' and 'virgin.'

Timothy was allowed to wear longers, jeans brought from England, by visiting friends. On his wall he put a picture that he got from a newspaper, of a showband singer with shirt open to the waist, surrounded by adoring women. He heard his parents muttering about it. His mother came in and told him to take it down.

'But why?'

'Because it's *unsuitable*.'

At the barbers, Timothy waited, and watched the goldfishes in the aquarium swimming around their green castle and in and out of caves, checking pebbles with their lips. One of them was trailing a little banner of fish shit. It was wonderful the way bubbles zhooshed up from under a rock. He would have liked to wait longer to look at them more, but there was no one else ahead of him.

'Can I have a Beatles haircut please.'

'You haven't got enough hair for that.'

He lived alone in his imagination, dreaming by the fireplace, where the coal was always forming little volcanoes with tarry lava oozing, in marvellous canyons of red and orange flame. He liked to heat the poker till it was red hot and burn holes into the lino with it. Only when his legs got so hot that they developed ABC's, would he move away from the fire, and then back when they disappeared.

He had still not made the connection between the secret pleasure he was obtaining, and anything else he had ever heard of. He was peeping through the window, lying on his bed one evening when he saw a girl being whirled around by somebody in one of the neighbouring gardens. As her feet rose from the ground and her dress billowed, he could see that she had no knickers on. It seemed somehow disgusting, exciting and fascinating all at once. Later the memory could be used to intensify the pleasure as he rubbed himself against the sheets. But it did not make him want her at all, just the memory.

By the time he started secondary school, Timothy had progressed beyond the watery stage and it was getting more difficult to continue the sliding technique, with his ever-increasing rigor and growing body. He still used the old method to get started. Sometimes he could eke out the fantasy to finish this way – still the best. He had to rack his memory for erotic incidents to enhance the experience but soon exhausted them all and had to turn to books for more inspiration. He knew there was a Harold Robbins somewhere in the house and he could find it, with a picture of a naked woman viewed from behind, seated at her dressing table. Harold Robbins was a celebrity in The News of The World, which came into the house on Sundays, with its blacked-out sections for the Irish edition.

The picture was enough in itself, but there were also parts of the text where a rape might be described; or anything referring to woman's anatomy could set him off, even a horrific reference to a squaw's breast turned into a tobacco pouch. If his penis got too hard for sliding, he would turn over and switch to the hand method. Then he would turn sideways and let the semen spill into the white cotton sheet. He was now up to two or three times a day, and still reaching new highs regularly. The problem became folding the sheets to avoid the sodden patch. It would be starched dry in the morning, and could be passed off as the result of a wet dream if necessary. When he heard the other boys talking in the locker room about wet dreams, Timothy wondered what it would be like to have one.

The only embarrassing thing was the creaking of the bed. The quieter he tried to be, the more little noises it seemed to make. He always imagined his family all lying there awake, hearing every creak and knowing exactly what it meant. But nothing was going to stop him now. Not even the acne, that the advice books said was nothing to do with masturbation, even though the evidence of his eyes showed him that the number of pimples was directly proportional to the amount of wanking.

There was only so much mileage in memories of self-exposure and glimpses under girls' skirts; and there was a limited supply of suitable books, though some champion ones provided months of hand-galloping material. Timothy's first favourite was 'Not as a Stranger' by Morton Thompson. He felt a sense of achievement after reading it, because it was long and serious, a 'real' book. There was a scene where the doctor examined a woman to determine pregnancy and knew partly by the brownish tinge in the areolas around her nipples. The idea of this examination took a long time to exhaust as a fantasy.

He found that the book 'In Praise of Older Women' contained plentiful resources for his purpose. To feed the ever-increasing demands of fantasy, he then began to imagine a neighbour's wife who had some kind words for him, behaving like one of the women in the book. Any woman who made contact and had a conversation with him, could be imagined opening her legs and wanting Timothy's hands on her, rustling the nylon between her thighs and in under her pants. She would want him to penetrate her, and it was on the moment of entering that he would come, not after the boring, laborious grind that might follow. He compared each new orgasm, and often afterwards repeated to himself that the latest one was the best ever.

There had to be plausibility for the fantasy to work, and it had to be timed to perfection. New record-breaking orgasms were becoming harder to obtain. A little distraction, such as the sheet slipping at the last minute, could ruin it. Any idea of implausibility that entered his mind would be even worse. After exhausting believable scenarios with Mrs A, he would switch to imagining what could happen with Mrs B. Only one or two of them offered any hint of realism. Some of them required too great a suspension of disbelief to be much use, and could not be made attractive. The only element of appeal that really mattered, though, was sheer availability. It helped if they were not completely gross, but that could be outweighed by seeming availability or apparent interest in sensual pleasure.

II

When Timothy was fifteen, he took a summer job helping the local breadman with deliveries. The breadman liked women who giggled, it was so feminine he thought. So the breadman was more than fond of Mrs C in the last block, who always came to the door in her very negligible negligee and who giggled continuously. He would spend quite a while there at the end of their rounds while Timothy did the last few flats. In the middle of their rounds there was another woman that he lunched with, in the eight-storey blocks, while Timothy worked. But the days began at Mrs Bacon's place in the flats on the other side of the estate. That was where they would meet up before starting their rounds. The breadman would usually be frying eggs, flipping oil onto them with the fishslice. Mrs Bacon would be sitting at the table, eating one of their Viennese fingers or coffee slices. By night, in his mind, Timothy pleasured all the lonely housewives of the bread round, one by one, the way that Yeats favoured wine – just the vapour, the angels' share.

Carrying panniers of bread and cakes, one on each arm, up and down stairwells made him strong. He was allowed to have his first go at driving the bread van, ran it up onto the kerb and nearly crashed it, but the breadman only laughed. At the end of the week, Timothy would make the payment collections in his local area. One or two of his friends began to accompany him, and as soon as they had enough money, they bought cigarettes and yoghurt or bottles of cream to drink, from the broken-down van that served as the local shop.

'There's nothing like the real thing,' one of them called Jack said. Jack claimed he had been staying at his older married brother's house, and walked into the wrong bedroom one night after a few drinks. When he got into the bed in the dark his sister-in-law mistook him for his brother. So he shagged her and crept out again, leaving nobody any the wiser. The story was too good to question, it was followed by a long silence. Nobody really believed Jack, but they were seized by a mystical fervour for 'the real thing.'

It was a time when girls were paired with boys in some instinctive way by the neighbourhood friends, after try-outs of kissing in party games, or along anonymous lines in the unlit, leaky garages under the flats. It was like picking teams for football, or seeding a tennis tournament. They assigned Timothy a girl called Joanna, a prize because she was said to be the only one who French kissed. She was a ballet dancer, with straight brown hair in a pageboy style, and dark brown eyes. Timothy had long hair, and pale blue eyes. He fell for her one day when he and she were talking on the corner. There was something in the way her eyes met his, and he said, 'Do you feel we have a certain rapport?' She was a little surprised, but not embarrassed. 'Yes, I feel that,' she said.

The Sunday the girls decided to go with the boys to stock car racing was a day of full summer sun. The boys led the way over a stone wall and through a woodland demesne. They walked all the way through the trees till they entered a field of tall golden wheat, where the girls lagged behind whispering and laughing. A wooden bridge over a drainage ditch led into another huge field. Through a gap in the hedgerow on the far side, they reached the back of the crude stock car racing track and bunked in under a wire fence. They dispersed and regrouped again, bought ice pops and watched while the numbered and painted shells of cars raced, and wrecked. All the time there was loud and mostly unintelligible commentary from a three-horned public address system on the grass in the middle of the track.

After the intensity and noise of the racing, on their way back some of the couples lay down in the hayfield. The sun was still high and hot. Timothy and Joanna kept walking till they were on their own in the woods. 'Do you want to stay here for a while?' he said. They sat down under a tree together, where easily and naturally he kissed her. It was true, her mouth was a cave, so he made his mouth like a cave too. They joined their caves for a while then followed their friends along the track and back over the stone wall.

That night on his own, her tongue met his. Her left hand went to his trousers and rubbed there. He turned and straightened to make himself feel bigger to her. His right hand slipped under her dress, between her thighs till his fingers found the boundary of nylon. She pressed and pressed on him through the jeans, and the more she pressed the more he felt the way he always wanted to feel; and the harder she pressed the more he thought to himself, truly, there is nothing like the real thing.

Beacon and Numbskull

Nick was standing in line to check-out some Indian vegetarian food for his lunch. Living alone and working from his house, he made a point of getting out daily to buy provisions. It was the last day of October, and the local High Street was full of late harvest fare.

'Numbskull!' the cashier said, with a big smile.

'Oh! You must have seen my picture online.'

'It's me, Beacon!'

'Beacon! Well I'll be damned... You're so different than I imagined, Beacon.'

'You mean you never knew I was black?'

Nick blushed.

'No, I mean you're absolutely beautiful!'

Rather glowing black with purple tones, than pink with hairy goosebumps, he thought. Other customers were waiting to be served.

'Look, I can see that this will take more than a quick chat to sort out,' she said, 'Meet me in the Tapas bar next door at 7 o'clock tonight and we'll have a good old chinwag.'

They had always exchanged glances whenever Nick bought something in the health food shop, and he always hoped their hands would touch when he paid.

Tonight would be Nick's first date since his wife had gone off with Mr Chicken. She had been Mr Chicken's secretary at corporate headquarters in the arsehole of the East End.

Something Beacon said about the décor in the Tapas bar, while they speared olives and whitebait over a pitcher of sangria, made Nick wonder if two people could ever truly agree on anything. She described the yellow walls as restful.

'People usually think green is restful, but for me yellow is the most relaxing,' she said. 'Green is oppressive.'

'That's interesting,' he said, 'because I'm the same with blue and red. I find blue warm, and red cold.'

'No, no! Blue is dull and boring,' she said. 'Red is intellectual and vibrant.'

'Isn't lilac intellectual,' said Nick, 'and grey boring?'

'Oh no,' said Beacon, 'grey is electrifying!'

'Let me just double-check here,' Nick said, laughing, 'you are female?'

'No,' said Beacon.

'Don't do that to me, Beacon! What is your real name, anyway?'

When Beacon finished laughing her head off, she said, 'Jacintha. What's yours?'

'Nick. Very boring, I'm afraid. Not like your exotic name.'

'P-lease? "Jacintha" is a very boring name. And *you* are colour-blind, my friend.'

'No not at all, I agree on the names of all the colours. Just the names, though.'

Jacintha made the sign of a jet plane flying over her head.

'You're Numbskull alright – I'm definite now. – Sorry, Nick.'

Their way home was the same as far as Jacintha's place, so it was natural for him to walk her there. The night had turned cold and misty. He was hoping she might offer the cup of coffee that keeps you awake, then lets you escape back to your own world after a few orgasms and a fry-up. Instead when they got to Jacintha's block, she gave him a peck on the cheek, said 'Goodnight' and disappeared like a breeze.

Out of the fog, a group of Halloween children appeared, dressed as witches and ghosts. 'Trick or Treat!' they cried, and rattled their collection tins as he climbed the hill to his house. Their leader was as tall as Nick and wore a Scream mask.

'It's past your bedtimes,' he answered, beside his gate.

The house was dark ahead of him. The four lingered nearby in their ugly masks.

'Clear off!' he said.

When he turned his back on them, he thought he heard one say, 'You had your choice!' When he looked around, they were gone.

He went inside and turned on his computer. It was the first thing Nick always did because it took so long to start up, and he wanted to check his messages as soon as possible. Then he went around the house drawing the curtains. Nick liked to close the curtains before turning on the lights, so as not to make a shop window for the nosey neighbours.

As he entered the dark living room, something outside approached the window, spangled by moonlight through the birch hedge. If it was a person, it was horribly misshapen, with its head on the wrong way. Pins and needles flushed Nick's limbs, as he tried to make sense of the looming presence. Maybe it was some trick by the Halloween children. No, it was more sinister. The figure moved again, then Nick remembered – it was only a potted plant he had moved closer to the house to protect it from frost.

Okay, he could go over to the window. A night storm had blown up. In the sudden gale the brown paper leaves of the birch hedges were rattling, their shadows trembling on the living room wall. Pressed behind the glass, was the Scream mask. Nick emitted an incoherent shout. The image disappeared.

'Bloody Screamer!'

Just when he recovered enough to continue pulling the curtains, an egg crashed on the window and slid down the outside of the glass.

Livid, Nick completed his round of darkened rooms

in the house, closing all the curtains and turning on a few lights. From the study a voice said, 'You have email.'

It was a message from Beacon. 'Happy Halloween,' it said, 'and thanks for an interesting evening. Let's do it again sometime!'

'Jacintha,' he typed, 'yes, it was lovely. Halloween! I've just been Tricked by the Trick-or-Treaters. They scared the crap out of me. I'll post full details online tomorrow. – Numbskull.'

As he clicked Send, there was a loud hammering at the front door, like a policeman's knock. It was followed by scuffing and running sounds. They had played another trick on him. Raging, he grabbed his house keys, rushed to the hall door and opened it. Most of the streetlights were out of order but he could see the Trick or Treaters lit by the moon in a vortex of cloud. They turned and ran. Nick launched himself from the doorstep and ran after them.

They were fitter than him. About halfway down the hill they scattered into the grounds of the building that Jacintha had gone into earlier. Nick followed the one with the Scream mask into a stairwell and up some steps that reeked of urine. 'They always go up, that's how they get caught,' he thought. He reached the top of the four-storey block. The Screamer, in a black robe was beside a door at the end of the landing holding a bunch of keys.

Before the Screamer could find the right key, Nick

was there, grabbed the robe and swung him. The Screamer fell and cracked the back of his head on the concrete balcony. Lights came on in a flat at the other end of the landing. The neighbours, an old couple, peeped round their door and quickly went back in. The Screamer was not moving.

'You stupid bastard! Are you okay?'

There was no answer. All blood drained from Nick's skin. To help the Screamer, he would have to remove the mask. The reaction to the chase hit Nick as he bent down. He started gasping for air. The same flush of pins and needles raced through his limbs again. 'Best tear it off quickly like a Band Aid,' he thought.

He forced himself to grasp the mask. It rose in his hand. Underneath, a blood-red Shinto demon turned and sneered at him. With a jolt like an electric shock, pain began to crush Nick's ribcage. The Shinto demon turned into a summer-blue Bambi cartoon, and then into the face of Jacintha, flicking her pink tongue around her lips. Unable to breathe, Nick buckled and fell on his knees, catching the edge of the robe.

The air was still acrid from bonfires and damp with mist when Jacintha opened her door in the morning. On the balcony outside her flat she found Numbskull lying dead on the robe, with a Scream mask in his hand.

Kenny

He came in from a jumble sale one Saturday morning, carried in a rusty old birdcage by my wife and son. No doubt some old dear had been separated from him, either by the Grim Reaper or the Social Services.

'Oh no you don't!'

'Don't worry, we'll look after it,' they said.

'Well you better, because I'm not cleaning out the cage!'

'What will we call him?'

'Kenny,' I said. It was clear that resistance was going to be futile. 'Kenny the Canary.'

As expected, I was the one who had to look after him: clean out his cage every week, replenish the water and birdseed every day. I used to seal up the room and let him fly around, at first, but the job of catching him again was such that he could not have enjoyed his excursions very much.

Kenny never did trust me though. I got off on the wrong foot with him, and nothing in nature knows more about right and wrong feet than a caged bird. I couldn't wait to see him take a birdbath in his new little plastic cage accessory. Several times I caught him and forced him into it. Naturally he was in terror of this experience. Then I always wanted him to eat out of my hand, but he never would come and take food unless I moved more than arm's length away from the cage.

So I played a waiting game. Every day I would change the water in the birdbath. Still he never used it. Instead, no matter what I tried, he would wash himself in the drinking water container, dipping down and fluttering the water all over.

The old cage was replaced with a bigger one. I still felt sorry for him and would have freed him, if it had been possible for him to survive on his own. Then a friend wanted to get rid of a female canary and gave it to us. We put Hillary, the new arrival, into the same cage with Kenny. That was a big mistake; canaries do not like to share their space. They come together to mate and then split the scene.

Hillary was bigger than Kenny, but she had a sore leg. As it got better, she became more and more aggressive to Kenny. She would attack him ferociously and he would back off. One day, I saw him standing down the bottom of the cage in a corner panting – as much as a tiny bird can pant – while Hillary sat on the top perch.

'She's going to kill him,' I thought. So I had to give Hillary back to where she came from. I heard later that she had escaped.

After that, Kenny was a new bird. He was chirpier than ever. I made a point of hanging his cage out on the rotary clothesline in the garden whenever the sun came out. He would warble vigorously, hop from perch to perch and catch the odd fly that happened by.

I would watch him from the window for ages. He was so happy, he would loop the loop – flying off a perch, looping around in the air and back again. I fed him aniseed scented seed sprays from one of the shrubs in the garden. One time I thought I had killed him when he collapsed into a birdie coma on the floor of the cage after eating some elderberries that I gave him. But he came round again.

His biggest scare was still to come. One day, my son said 'Dad, there's a big ugly bird standing on the shed, looking at Kenny.' I went to the window. It was a sparrowhawk. I started out to the garden quickly to take Kenny's cage in. By the time I got down the steps, the sparrowhawk had launched itself at the cage and smashed itself into it.

It continued to batter at the cage until I was nearly there, with a violence that I have never seen equalled, before giving up and flapping out of sight. It had actually prised two of the bars apart. Kenny did not seem too bothered. He hopped around – but he had no tail whatsoever. The sparrowhawk had pulled his tail off. It grew back eventually.

The greatest thing was when I started to notice that the birdbath had been used. (I was still setting it up for him in the hope that he might use it eventually.) There were a couple of yellow feathers in there and the water was dirty. So I spied on him now and then, until eventually I got to see him go into the birdbath, stand in the water, and toss it up over himself, fluttering and ending up soaking wet. Joy! Many times, after that, he would be so wet that he would miscalculate his flight, miss a perch and fall down. But he soon dried out.

He even began to let me come closer, though he never did eat right out of my hand. I think he would have eventually, had time allowed. The key thing was for me not to bother him. The more I left him alone, the more he trusted me.

After a few years, it happened that Kenny started to stay on the floor of his cage all the time. We wondered if he was ill, but thought the trauma of a visit to the vet might finish him off altogether. We just assumed that he was suffering from old age. I lowered all three perches and the cuttlefish bones he used to stand on, so that they were all near the bottom of the cage. It helped – he would use the lowest one. But one day he would not even get on the lowest perch.

I was so worried about him, I moved him to the sunniest spot in the house, even though the cage would be obstructing the hallway. He stopped preening himself and looked a sad figure. He no longer had any fear of me now and came right up to take food. But mostly he just stood alone, panting.

I came down one morning and he was lying on the

floor of the cage. When I went to tell my wife, it came hard to say, 'I think Kenny is dead.' Half hoping he might revive, like the time after eating the elderberries, I left him there till the next day. Eventually he was buried in a little herbal tea box, under a tree at the bottom of the garden, and covered over with stones. I like to think that Kenny is somehow reincarnated into the wild songbirds that play in his tree and fly away.

Holy Orders

The sea is like a drug. Lifting the ferry high then letting go. Dropped, she dashes down. The swell bears her up again, bow into the night. In the lounges, migrants are rocked to sleep by the droning turbines.

He wrestles the hatch open and steps into the roar. The engines are throbbing above the white noise of wind and water. All about the closeting dark. Not a flickering buoy or star.

For Father Frank Hardiman, reminders of passion in the bucking haunches of the Irish sea. He is sailing home from his lifetime mission among the heathen English. Behind him their voices die like gulls on a tip. Before him the Atlantic-hammered moans of the faithful beckoning as to St. Patrick.

A poloneck sweater and two days' stubble are as nothing in the icy blast. The deep flicks and rolls him like a cigarette to be crushed in a crowd. Booms of white hair pivot on the deck of his head, ebb and flow like seaweed on a wrinkled shore. His coat is a black cylinder down to his Doc Marten's boots.

What it is to be pitched onto the high sea. So soon after dozing in his study in Wembley, in the afternoon's simmering torpor, to the hum of Mrs Haverty's hoover.

'Excuse me. Excuse me,' a voice started. 'Can I hold your hand for a minute?'

A rhetorical question — she was already linking him on the darker, shipward side. A current of fear made the hair on the back of his head stand on end. Pale electric light bulged from the lounge as a young man in army surplus stepped out and approached them warily.

He peered in their direction for a moment coming over. He was crookbacked with a thin face and wiry hair. Hardiman's anxiety abated seeing the stature of the pursuer. It shrunk further when the stranger spoke in a self-pitying whine.

'Esther! For the love of God. I only want to talk to you.'

'I told you before, my name is not Esther. This man is a nutcase. He's been following me ever since we got on in Holyhead, raving about this Esther.'

'Esther, if you do this to me,' the man pointed at her, 'I can't be responsible for what I do. Now will you come with me or not?'

Hardiman could feel the waif shudder as she clung more tightly to his arm.

'Just go away, this lady doesn't want you here. If you don't go away,' his voice climbed, 'I'll report you—' At that moment the ship's foghorn sounded, drowning the man's reply. The man grinned for no apparent reason, turned around and went back inside.

The girl was shaking, whether from cold or sobbing. There was not much of her face to be seen as her straight black hair covered one side and she looked down shyly. She had on a voluminous jacket over a skimpy vest. Her trousers were baggy, all straps and pockets, and she wore small shoes with no socks as far as he could see.

'Let's go inside,' he shouted when it started raining. They sat across a table in the dozing lounge amid mumbling insomniacs. He felt a resurgence of the sea-sickness which had prompted him to go on deck in the first place. The muffled drumming of the engines, the ship rolling and smells of milky tea and evaporating beer began to tell in the hue of his skin.

'I'm sorry, what is your name?' he began, 'I know it's not Esther.'

'Gail'

'I'm afraid I'm feeling ill, Gail. I hope you don't mind if I retire to my cabin at this, eh, juncture. If you have any more trouble, I suggest you approach some of the crew.' He waited with increasing discomfort for any sign of an answer.

'I don't suppose you have a berth?'

She shook her head, still wearing the same shame-faced look.

He rose against the sway of the ship and was halfway to his cabin before he realised that she was following him. He felt even sicker and began to blame the turn of events for the turn of his stomach.

She stood behind him when he opened the door on the cramped quarters. It was like a walk-in closet or glorified locker. Her presence could not deflect him in his rush to rest away nausea on the bunk.

'Do you mind?' she pleaded.

He knew the lower in the ship you go the less it sways, so he was going to take the bottom bunk. He crumpled forward, mumbling 'You're welcome to the top bunk if you want it.' He closed his eyes. 'Please don't talk or say anything. I can't deal with it right now.'

The double bunks filled one half of the cabin. In the corner behind the door was a tiny enamel sink. She dropped a holdall on the floor and kicked off her shoes to climb to the upper bunk. His nausea sensitised him to the vinegar scent of her feet as they bent round the rungs of the small ladder that passed near his face. He listened to the faint creaking sounds as she settled in.

'Goodnight,' he said.

He was woken by a surge of clangour from children of families in the surrounding cabins. Gail had flown. Going up on deck he saw the distant lights of Dublin in the early dawn. A few gannets followed the ferry swooping for pieces of garbage from a bucket, where a seaman far below was emptying it over the stern rail.

He went to the self-service restaurant to get some coffee and toast. While queuing he reached inside his black clerical jacket for his wallet, but it was gone. He pushed his way back through the herding passengers with such force that somebody swore at him, priest or not.

Father Frank Hardiman waited on the upper deck for the Leyland bus to move off on its dawn run into Amiens Street. Under grey sky a blustery, salty wind scoured the lifeless container port. Gasworks and sea smells came in atomised drizzle through the rickety bus window above him.

He was on his way to the presbytery of his one-time colleague Tony Dowell. O temple of ideals! They flocked there from the ends of the parish to sing Eric Clapton songs and write free verse. They never were able to tune those guitars but it didn't seem to matter. Father Anthony's door was always open. Or if not, you just had to knock and it would be opened unto you.

He got off the bus and walked down Talbot Street past knocking shop hotels and dirty, shuttered hucksters' shops, to get another bus. Under the railway bridge, he noticed MacHugh Himself was still there, and the Educational Book Company. He wondered if everything would've changed, but nothing had. A van from the Swastika Laundry of Rialto was the only traffic. He didn't think that brand would've survived. It had been twenty years since he left Dublin in 1979.

He was the only passenger on the number forty to Finglas village. Predominance of tarmac and grass. As the bus struggled uphill, protesting plane trees sprang their bare branches – thwack – on the roof. By the time the bus reached the old village he was yawning.

He saw the familiar shape of the place, the edge of a plateau where the streets fell away suddenly to the west down into an old graveyard. He wondered if the cobbler's shop was still at the corner of the sunken Y junction below.

He only had a small Gladstone bag to carry up the hill when he got off. In it was a present for Tony Dowell, a box of incense granules for the church. It was Mrs Haverty who insisted he ought to bring something and there was nothing else to hand. It was short notice when the phone call came; his uncle had died, and would he come over for the funeral right away. Mrs Haverty wanted him to take the plane, but he couldn't stand flying. He'd have been sick and white-knuckled, and sure to bring bad luck on the plane. 'Don't worry, God,' he thought. 'I don't believe in superstition, I only practice it.'

He climbed up the hill to the parish church, a huge granite building which the faithful were still paying for in dues exacted weekly. He had hoped to become parish priest there, but Tony Dowell got it, and Hardiman ended up in London. He had taken a position as far away as he could, not wanting to play second fiddle to his old friend. He'd never gotten his own parish, but he no longer wanted one. All for a peaceful life.

The dead leaves were a foot deep by the garden walls of the presbytery. He kicked them a little for a lark. Hardiman let himself in, the lock was unchanged. Into the musty silence of the carpeted hall, came a muttering from upstairs. Father Dowell, in a bathrobe, nipped down the first decade of the stairs.

'Frank! Welcome! Make yourself at home. I'll be with you in a minute.'

'I'll carry my things upstairs out of the way.'

He heard Dowell's voice distantly from the bedroom saying not to bother. Hardiman assumed it was only for politeness. They'd lived in the house for a number of years before Dowell got the Parish, and Hardiman still felt at home there. It didn't look any smaller, it was still a big house. So he plodded up the stairs to settle his things into the guestroom ready for hanging. As he passed along the landing, the master bedroom door was ajar.

'Tony?' he began.

He paused for an instant and then opened the master bedroom door. There was a stocky, longhaired young lady dressing herself hurriedly. Dowell sat down on the bed, and put his head in his hands.

Before anybody could say 'I can explain,' Hardiman closed the door. He left his luggage in the guestroom and then retreated back down the stairs. As he switched on a tea kettle in the kitchen, he heard the lovers saying goodbye at the front door, and Dowell calling after her – of all things – 'Adieu!'

Red Dot on a Harbour Wall

I've been running all my life. I race from boulder to boulder randomly in this rocky desert. I don't know where it starts or ends. It might be an infinite maze. I am able to run very fast, as if I had a powerful engine propelling me.

It is important to race because there are only a few crumbs of food, say every few minutes. So I have to try and find them before the other red dots do.

I could tell you some crazy stories. I was abducted by aliens one day and carried into space, on a smooth, slightly convex plane. It was mostly pink with a white half-moon shape before a ridge at one end. There was nobody else aboard, as far as I could see. They lowered me back into the endless rocky desert a little later.

I've seen spirits with wings, some benign, some murderous, all ugly. Oh yes. I've seen other beautiful red dots eaten alive by flying devils, or swallowed by huge monsters with hard beaks instead of mouths.

It's not easy being a red dot.

II

All Those Endearing Young Charms

The End

Hostel

Tunnel! Forget your shame, your degradation. Let the sound of the train be a machine gun cutting you down. Light again! Shut your eyes.

He had landed at Dover, carried along in a slow-moving crowd. A uniformed man stamped his Irish passport. The money went quickly in Paris, even living on croque monsieur and draft beer. He had a room under the roof of a pension near the Place d'Italie. At night the spring fragrance of the city filled the room through the open window, bearing traces of Turkish tobacco and lady of the night.

Tunnel! Remember the presents you bought her. She rejected them. Rattle that gun! Let it cut you down. Light! The sound of a sabre as it beheads you is the word, 'Forget.'

England is not black and white, the News of the World

is wrong. Everywhere smells of pine disinfectant. It is swathed in scrub, and hardy weeds. Into Victoria station in the early morning. He goes to the guard's van for the bike. After the train empties, the guard walks along the platform shutting the slam doors.

Tunnel! Let the door slam you. To forget. Slam! Forget. Slam! Forget. Forget. Forget.

A million people arrive in Victoria, suited, tied and taciturn on the escalators at the same time as Joseph. One of them lies ashen on the concourse, suited, tied and dead. The million ignore him. They flow out of the underground and spill into the street.

He chains his bike to a railing in Bayswater, outside a hotel that advertised rooms for £16 a week in the evening paper. No thought of her in his head. One change of clothing in his bags. One week to get a job and avoid running home with his tail between his legs.

In the grubby hallway of the Haywain Hotel, a flaking, five-storey building on the corner of a railed square in Bayswater. The Reception must have been a cloakroom originally. Just visible above the counter is the bald head of a man with a permanent expression of distaste. A young French girl is checking out. With her baggage around her, there is no room for Joseph to enter.

'Avez vous le bon temps, oui?' The man is trying out his school French in a wheedling voice.

'Why you don't tell me there is someone telephone for me?' she asks.

'Peut etre you were not here, n'est-ce pas?'

She makes the sign of the loco to Joseph on her way out. Joseph checks in.

'You'll be sharing with three other geezers. £2 for the key – you get that back when you leave. I don't care what you do as long as you don't set fire to the place. The dining room is down the stairs behind the door at the end of the hall. The times are listed on the door. Be careful as you open the door not to fall down the steps.'

The room has four beds, a sink with a shaving mirror, and a boarded-up fireplace. On the mantelpiece there are alarm clocks and bottles of after shave. On the other side is a wardrobe. Opposite the door is a green painted sash window, opened up over the street below.

Tunnel! The green of her school uniform, when you first watched her on her way to school. Slam the sash window on your hands till all the red hope bleeds out of them.

'You've got the wrong room,' says a bony old man, propped up against pillows on a bed near the window.

'The key fits, and this is 29b isn't it?'

'The keys are all the same. So, you must be the new victim. They come and go.'

'I just came from Paris, on a bike. I'm from Dublin really.'

'A Paddy! Another Paddy!'

The old man pauses to cough, horribly.

'Sorry. You get used to calling everyone by their nationality here. Taffy, Jock – it's easier. You can't remember all their names. What's your name anyway John?'

'Joseph. Joseph Murphy.'

'Eddie Cullen, that's my name. I'm a Paddy too. Sixty years I've been here.'

'What part –'

'From Cork. All my people are in Cork. Never went back. Too expensive. Tell a lie – I went back once. It wasn't the same.'

He wheezes into another coughing fit.

From outside a voice calls, 'Eddie! Eddie! … Are you there Eddie?'

'Tell him I've gone out. I don't want to see him. Go on! Tell him I'm not here.'

Joseph leans over the window sill and looks down at the caller, a middle-aged man in a suit.

'He's not here!'

'Oh. When did he go out?'

'I don't know. Sorry, I've only just got here.'

In the laundrette around the corner, as he is putting his dirty clothes into a machine, Joseph sees the French girl he met checking out earlier. She's with some other girls, laughing and drinking cola while they wait for their washing. He has brought a book to read while waiting.

Tunnel! You tried to give her a book – expensive, she didn't want it. Forget!

The French girl makes the sign of the loco to him. Does she mean it is he who is mad? The washdrum turns. Later, after they leave, when he takes the clothes out of the machine, he realises that he has thrown the book in with them. 'Down and Out in Paris and London' is now a pulp novel.

Baker Street

Joseph emerges from the underground into the London night, and makes a call to Aidan in Dublin. 'Guess where I am?' He mimics a familiar saxophone riff into the phone, and pushes the door of the telephone booth open with his foot. *Baker Street.* He feels brave not asking after Deirdre.

But the voice from Dublin is already more than distant, as if there is nothing left to talk about. Joseph could say he sold his bike, but how could he convey the Saturday market at Portobello Road, the people, the railway arches where bikes were auctioned, the hostel, the bars, the underground, the fast-walking couples – so many things.

That night while he lay in the room where three other people were sleeping, Joseph began to let the memories return. There had been a summer rainstorm in the hollow of the village, the day they said goodbye. The damp got into the engine of his 2CV and it wouldn't start. With some friends she helped to push-start it, and watched him on his way with that double-edged smile of hers, half mockery, half admiration. He had built his hopes on the sand of that fleeting smile.

'All we had was sex,' she said. 'We were not married. I never said till death us do part!'

'You said you loved me. You can't take that away from me.'

'I never said that.'

'You did.'

'I never actually said those exact words.'

'And then you disappeared off to Majorca with a bloody artificial inseminator!'

'Artificial inseminator? Who – Rusty? Rusty is a steel erector.'

'A steel erector! A steel erector? Aidan told me he was an A.I. man. Anyway, he didn't last long. They don't last long.'

In spring as the apple blossom turned to confetti in the parish of St Francis, Joseph announced that he was leaving town. He wondered if it was true that she was seeing a staid civil servant, ten years her elder.

'Dowdy by name, and Dowdy by nature,' her brother Aidan had reported.

'Thanks,' Joseph called back from the bike, while Aidan watched him on his way.

It had been worth waiting in reception for hours before his ex-boss appeared and handed over the reference that he'd been promising for weeks.

'You can only go so far over there,' he had said. 'To them you'll always be just another Paddy.'

The reference turned out to be perfect. 'Ever sober, upright and late,' the boss joked, as he handed it to Joseph. The bike was outside reception, laden. Joseph had set off on it that morning as his mother and sisters waved goodbye following him to the corner of the street, while the local street kids looked on.

Sitting in the small office of Solomon and Son, Furriers, above Great Portland Street in London, wearing clothes that would not pass for presentable much longer, the reference was the thread by which Joseph's life hung. Solomon Junior held it, mouthing the words silently as he read. He was so impressed by Joseph and his amazing dream reference, that he advanced the cost of renting a bedsit.

Joseph went to meet Jimmy from St Francis school, who was also in London. They had a few Neutron Bombs in the Sicilian pub near Baker Street before dropping into somebody's place, a basement flat nearby. The room was dim under one of those giant paper lampshades. There was a saxophone on a stand and tall bongos on one side. It belonged to Henry, a suave, black pimp and wheeler dealer. They sat cross-legged in a circle and smoked dope from a water pipe.

'This is Joseph, be nice to him,' Jimmy said. 'He's a refined Dubliner – not like me. He pronounces all his THs.'

'How did you get on with Nisha,' Jimmy asked.

Nisha was a small, nubile Indian lady who helped Joseph find somewhere to stay. She walked him from her flat through the nearby park to Golders Green to look at newsagents' notice boards. They cut across the grass – it was June – and talked about how landlords didn't want tenants with children.

'It's not a problem for me,' she said, 'I have no maternal instinct whatsoever.'

They found a notice for him to follow up, £32 per week near Brent Cross station. She stood on tiptoe to kiss him goodbye.

'She was sweet, very open. I'm going to see her at some party. I think you're going too, aren't you?'

Jimmy got out a small ball of opium he'd brought in from Hong Kong, and they smoked it. He was a stocky, wire haired, hard man, who wore work overalls at all times.

It was late and Joseph had to go. Solomon Junior would be standing beside the door, crouched over his watch and tutting, 'You're two minutes late!' if he didn't make the race from the underground to the furriers dead on time.

Solomon Junior was tall, burly but stooped, with black hair and hangdog jaws. The father, who was equally tall but without the hunched shoulders, was afraid to retire. His hair was white from worry about his blustering son, whose behaviour he would frequently have to moderate with a few whispered words. Seldom did a day pass without a row, usually involving Solomon Junior causing the mousy accounts lady to weep.

Joseph rented a bedroom and upstairs kitchen in the house of a middle-aged, childless couple on the suburban side of Brent Cross. It was clean and smelled of nothing but soap. They said he was to be one of the family, as if you could get a family from an advertisement in a newsagent's window. Having just escaped from one family he had no intention of falling into another.

Blind Date

Every morning he stood on the sunny platform of Brent Cross station, and every morning there was a certain girl waiting for the same train. There seemed to be some sort of attraction between them though they never spoke. One Saturday in the Golders Green cinema he became convinced that she was somewhere in the rows behind him. How he knew this, was a mystery; but a powerful force seemed to lock him in her invisible gaze. After a few minutes she came and sat in the empty seat next to him, but he didn't dare speak to her and after a while she got up and left.

Joseph danced with Nisha at the party. She was

wearing a short leopard skin print skirt. His attention wandered when she was talking to him, and when he turned back he saw that she had left. He had thought he saw his sultry morning girl across the room, but it was someone else's girl with bedroom eyes. When going home time came it was too late for public transport, and girls had to be walked home. Joseph was left with a friend of Jimmy's called Connie.

Looking down into her eyes in the black of midnight, although he did not know it yet, he was doomed. It was like looking into a pint of Guinness – one too many or one at the wrong time. The night was as black as her Sobranie cigarettes, black as the little ball of opium that he smoked with Jimmy. Connie was not his magnetic dream girl, but out of politeness he walked her to the nurses' home in Bloomsbury. She gave him an old-fashioned kiss goodnight. All he could see were her eyes looking up at him under the streetlight.

'How will you get home?' she asked. 'You'll have to get a taxi.'

'Will one pound fifty be enough for a taxi to Brent Cross?'

He pictured the miles of beige-grey concrete empty in the night. It ended up with Connie leading the way upstairs into the nurses' home. They entered a tiny wedge-shaped room, with a sink by the foot of a single bed, and an old radiator. It was hot. She put a blanket down for him, and he tried to sleep there on the floor beside her bed. She said she was afraid of the dark, and left a red lava lamp on with a pair of black tights over it.

Before he could sleep her hand reached down to his, and he joined her in the bed. She helped him to mount her, and suffered his actions, with a condom numbing everything. In a while they did it again and twice more. After each time there were ablutions in the little sink at the foot of the bed in the red glow of the shaded lava lamp.

'Insert the rubbish in the bin,' she said.

In the cool Autumn morning, he slipped out of the nurses' home and walked up Oxford Street to work. He couldn't wait to tell someone all he'd heard about his exotic oriental princess, and her exalted family as he imagined them. It was as if he had been adopted by a royal clan. Both he and she were on the rebound. They talked about their old flames, and soon they talked of marriage. Every night they made love in the nurses' home and every morning he stole out and walked up cold, sunny Oxford Street to work – till one morning the janitor caught him.

Jimmy let them stay in a spare bedroom with the narrowest single bed ever made. It was in a basement flat in Pimlico. The box room was unheated and they clung together for warmth. Never having actually gone to sleep properly with someone before, he was startled when she spoke in her sleep, 'The procedure is called myringotomy,' she muttered.

He tried to imagine what it would be like in a few years with Connie, and thought to himself, yes a thousand years of this would be fine. To people who saw him he would have appeared to be in a detached and euphoric state. His eyes were like those of members of religious cults who proselytise in the street, pupils narrowed and minds fixed.

In the house where Jimmy had the basement flat, there was a vacant bedsit on the top floor. It overlooked a mews. The landlord was trying to clear the house and so the top floor was not let. They decided to stay in the empty room. Joseph dragged his luggage out of the Brent Cross bedsit when the unwanted middle-aged couple were out.

Connie got a printed tiger fur blanket and they convinced themselves that sleeping on the floor was good for their backs. The room had a gas fire, an Ascot 'geyser' over the sink for hot water and a cooker. The gas meter in the room was open, so one coin served forever and nobody came to collect. Their furniture was a borrowed small table and two discarded chairs picked up from the street.

Their mirror was a gift from one of Connie's ex-boyfriends. It was imprinted with a different sexual position to illustrate each sign of the Zodiac. They worked their way through the signs. He liked Scorpio, which involved carrying her, and she liked Virgo which involved nearly breaking him.

The room was under the roof of a once grand terraced house near the river, within the sound of Big Ben. Their neighbours in the other room on the top landing were a female couple from the Philippines. The girls' room had a bed, and a shrine decked out with candles and the Sacred Heart. In the middle of the shrine was a picture of a Home Office minister; to whom they were praying for permission to stay in the country.

The other floors of the house held a Spanish car mechanic and his family, an Italian waiter with a Filipina wife, a fat bloke from Belfast who worked security in a department store, and Jimmy with his West Indian girlfriend. They were all refugees of one kind or another, though what each was running from might take a lifetime to discover.

When Joseph took Connie to Dublin to show her off the following summer, she was already visibly pregnant. They traced the time of conception to one of their torrid nights on the tiger skin beside the gas fire. They had married on a whim during the winter, but they told each other that love had grown between them.

Refugees

In Tachbrook Street market on a Saturday in December, Joseph stood back from the stalls, admiring the steaming barrels of beetroot, lobsters twitching, all that exotic and everyday abundance arrayed there, but most of all Connie's command of shopping. No list was needed; she ordered her ingredients instinctively, as fast as they could supply, and human-chained them back in plastic carrier bags to him.

She would have carried more things if he let her, though their baby was already overdue. She selected the world's largest watermelon and the plastic carrier bags cut into his fingers. His only part in shopping was as a pack animal, to lug her chosen items.

After they returned from shopping, Connie was working at the tiny draining board beside the sink when what looked like a slew of black beetles came skittering across the floor.

'What the hell is that?' said Joseph. 'Are they cockroaches or something?'

'No – seeds from the watermelon.'

It was so ripe that when she slashed it the seeds flew out.

As usual they talked almost all night, or rather Connie talked and Joseph answered. It would take many years to bring him up to date, before he could ever sleep properly again. At one point he got up to get a drink of water and had to step over her.

'Don't you know you must never do that?' she complained.

'What?'

'It's bad luck to step over somebody, especially if they're pregnant.'

Next day she was checking into Westminster Hospital. He stayed with her all that Sunday, and they talked about names for the baby. He thought 'Mark' would be best, because it sounded hard. When Connie accepted his opinion easily, it made him feel like a grown man, almost for the first time.

That afternoon a nurse told them they were going to induce the birth. Connie was taken into the delivery room. Midwives were doing their thing, monitors were bleeping, and Joseph was doing the handholding, through four hours of pain.

'Can I have a word?' said the doctor, and ushered Joseph outside into the corridor. The doctor said it would be best to deliver the baby by caesarean section. The whole world disappeared, leaving only their two voices and shapes in the corridor.

'She wants to have it naturally. Is that not possible?'

But the baby's heartbeat was beginning to indicate distress, the doctor said, and he thought an operation would be safer for both mother and child.

'I can only go by what you say. I just don't know. If you're sure it's for the best?'

'Yes. Would you have a word with her, and reassure her?'

They went back inside.

'I don't want to. I don't want to. I don't care how long it takes.'

'The doctor says it's for the best,' he told her.

She grasped his hand tightly.

'It's up to you. Will you let them?'

She puckered her mouth and eyebrows like a child about to weep, and nodded agreement with a whimper. He looked at the doctor. She fretted fearfully, squeezing his hand until he had to let go as they wheeled her away.

Knowing that your wife is being C-sectioned and your baby being born, you do not wait like a bored visitor. You pace, you picture the surgery as clearly as if you were in there with them. You check for news from any passing nurses. The time seems to go very quickly. After about ninety minutes a team appeared with a small transparent cot on a trolley. A man in a white coat said, 'Congratulations, you have a baby boy! Don't worry, Consuelo is doing fine.' They stopped to let him look.

'Is he okay?' was Joseph's question.

'Yes.' said the man.

'He has all his little bits and pieces,' added another nurse.

His baby is here, five minutes old with gauze gloves and black spiky hair. He is looking straight at his father. Joseph says 'Hello,' and the baby makes a noise as if to answer.

When Connie comes back from theatre, she is too shattered to mind the baby. Her caesarean wound is stapled. Mother and child are put in the recovery room together. Joseph wants to hold Connie's hand, but it looks painful with a drip in place. She reached out, but now she has fallen asleep. He pulls up an armchair and tries to stay overnight with them. After midnight one of the nurses insists on taking the chair away and makes him go home.

It is the third week of December. Joseph still has to work up to the Christmas holiday. When he shows a picture of his newborn baby to Solomon Junior all he says is 'Well you have a Chinese baby!' and hands it back.

The hospital has decided to keep Connie in for a few days because her wound has developed an infection. After work, he walks from Pimlico across Vauxhall Bridge Road and down through the red brick canyons of the Peabody buildings. A sleety north wind steals through the playgrounds and high railings. He is still wearing summer clothes, because money is tight.

When Christmas Eve comes the infection is no better. Connie and the baby have to stay in hospital over the holiday. The doctor says it's unlikely she can have any more children. The fathers are allowed to stay late tonight. Near midnight, the ward sister turns down the lights and a choir processes around the ward carrying candles for torches, and begins to sing God Rest Ye Merry Gentlemen.

On Christmas morning, a visiting colleague of Connie's brings the baby a toy music box, a blue plastic cube that winds up with a pull-string. They are in a public ward, with baby Mark in his Perspex cot, busily kicking off his coverlets already. At the other end of the bed, Connie is chatting with her visitor. Joseph pulls out the string of the music box, which is hanging on the side of the cot, and an unfamiliar tune begins to play.

The song must have started in the wrong place, only now he recognizes it.

Believe me if all those endearing young charms
Which I gaze on so fondly today...

Alone as he watches his son shadow boxing to the music, from a deep wellspring a few tears overflow, the silent kind that only know themselves why they flow. Something has been completed, something has been lost, and a new life begun.

Moonshine

I

It was a hot afternoon in summer. Deirdre was far enough down the garden to forget about the house, and it was secluded enough there that nobody could see her in her swimsuit. She turned onto her back on the lounger and put on her sunglasses.

In the cool on the other side the house, lace curtains billowed from an open window. Deirdre's brother Frank put one of his Lennon records on loud. On the kerbside, trees in full leaf extended the shade of the front gardens. Across the concrete road, heat shimmered on the green. The first few piano chords of the record were joined by the sound of a car approaching.

People say we've got it made.

Don't they know we're so afraid? – Isolation.

Deirdre heard the car pull up outside and somebody getting out. Her brother Aidan was talking to someone. Damn! He would take over 'his' garden now. The record stopped. She could hear Frank greeting a surprise visitor and wondered who it was.

'Come through, come through!' said Aidan. 'This is what I've been working on – my pride and joy.'

He was showing his guest the garden.

'See, there are three sections. This first one is the vegetable patch. It's for some strange peasants who live here. They call themselves my parents.'

'To remind them of their roots,' said the guest.

'Oh no – the puns!' Aidan laughed, and backed through the vine-swathed arch in the trellis. The visitor followed.

'Now this is my little sister, Deirdre. I'm sure you must remember her!' said Aidan.

'Of course, how could I forget!'

She looked up, raised her sunglasses and recognised Joseph Murphy. He had changed from the shy, long-haired adolescent she remembered from a few years ago.

Aidan said, 'I met this guy getting into a car downtown and cadged a lift.'

Joseph was now lean and self-possessed. She noticed his steel-blue eyes. Most of the young men she met fell into one of two categories: uncouth opportunists or hapless wimps, and she was able to classify them instantly, but she was not sure about this one.

While her brother and his guest explored the garden, she slipped away. Upstairs in her back bedroom, their conversation drifted through the open window, while she put on her clothes.

'So what are the broads like in the factory?' How typical of Aidan to ask like that.

'They're all scrubbers,' Joseph was saying, ' – in short. I don't actually get to meet them; they are in a different place. I work in the storeroom and the cutting room where it's all blokes, unfortunately. I tell a lie! There is one girl who fancies me but unfortunately she's epileptic and tends to faint when I talk to her. I shouldn't make fun of her.'

'Of course you should!' said Aidan.

When Deirdre came downstairs and looked in the kitchen door, her younger brother Frank was standing inside laughing over their unexpected guest. Aidan was making tea, and cutting up one of the homebaked apple pies that had given the kitchen its stale, homely smell over the years. Joseph was sitting at the table.

'Is that your heap of junk outside or should I get it towed away?' joked Frank.

Deirdre came and stood near Frank, her green corduroy jeans tight around her thighs, and gingham blouse with a couple of buttons undone at the neck. She had soft, fair hair, half waist length and with a fringe. There was a hint of something embattled in her features. She looked down on Joseph with a mixture of amusement and mock contempt.

'Do you still write songs?' her brother Frank asked Joseph, in a voice hoarse with suppressed mirth and mild amazement.

'Not much. Now and again,' said Joseph.

'I remember you playing your guitar in the basement of the flats and singing.'

'It was all rubbish,' said Joseph.

The street children used to be amazed to hear Joseph's self-penned songs in the open basements of the system-built flats, on a guitar with strings missing. The flats had open, garage-like basements that were used for handball, smoking, graffiti, and unofficial public toilets. It was not the quality of Joe's compositions that impressed people, it was the mere fact somebody was standing in the middle of a pissy concrete basement, and hammering out something new.

'We thought you were brilliant.'

'No.'

Joseph blushed and could not think what else to say.

'Cheers anyway, see ya!' said Frank in a rising tone, and went out.

On his way out the front door, Frank let in Deirdre's friend Rosaleen. Aidan was turning on the transistor radio on the window sill in the kitchen when Rosaleen came in, and it started playing *Push push in the bush*. Rosaleen said she wondered what that was all about, and the two girls laughed, shoulder to shoulder.

Rosaleen was slender with high cheekbones and black hair in a French bob. Joseph told her, 'You'd be the image of Debbie Harry if you dyed her hair blonde.'

'Is that a compliment,' she said, 'I don't think so.'

'It's meant to be,' he said.

Aidan said, 'We're going to Joseph's place for a drink. Do you two want to come?'

Deirdre exchanged questioning looks with Rosaleen. It was agreed. Joseph and Aidan took the front seats in the old 2CV, and the girls got in the back. The car had a dashboard shift.

'My mother thought it was an invalid car,' said Joseph, 'but didn't like to say.'

They left the avenues of purchase houses behind. Twilight was turning to night as they drove through the estate surrounded by system-built concrete flats, to the Dublin Corporation house where Joseph's family were tenants.

It was for the bottle of whiskey they had come, of which they all now sipped, except Deirdre who was tee-total. Aidan chatted eagerly and joked, with often blurted laughter that lit-up his hangdog, five-o-clock-shadowed face.

'Now this is not mine – honest!' Joseph protested, as stylus hit vinyl and the Stylistics began.

God bless you

You make me feel brand new

Aidan started dancing with Rosaleen. Following their lead, Deirdre danced with Joseph, hugging closely. Joseph nestled on her shoulder breathing the softness of her hair and warmth of her body. Aidan was livelier in his dance moves, with a cheerful, workmanlike approach as the four of them danced around the small parlour. Deirdre and Joseph were still slow-dragging and The Stylistics were played over again after Rosaleen and Aidan returned to their drinks.

On their way back home, Deirdre sat in front with Joseph.

'I'll see you tomorrow,' said Rosaleen when she got out, looking in the open window of the passenger door at Deirdre and, turning to Aidan, joked, 'I think we better leave these two love birds!'

When they were alone, Joseph asked if he could see her again. Deirdre agreed and they exchanged a chaste kiss, with just a hint of cool moisture between their lips.

Deirdre double-dated Joseph with Rosaleen and Aidan, the first few times. The time they went out on their own, it was to see Pasolini's 'One Thousand and One Nights' at the IFT. She was inflamed by the erotic scenes. That night outside her house their kisses were passionate, but Deirdre pulled away.

'They'll see us.'

So they drove a little way beyond where the suburb met the first fields, and parked in a layby. She moved for him, and her hand followed his as they tested the fabric between them, till she said, 'It's late, we better go.'

He was so distracted when they kissed goodnight that he let her go without making another date. She was glad. He wanted to see her every day, but she liked to keep some days for herself.

When she let herself in, her father was smoking his

pipe and reading a newspaper. Her mother was already in bed and the brothers were watching a spaghetti western on TV.

'I hope there's a psycho in this,' Frank was saying. 'I love psychos!'

Deirdre went straight upstairs and ran a bath. Her vision was blurring. She looked into the mirror to see her eyes, but couldn't focus clearly. As she sank down in the bathwater, she was aware of her limbs losing sensation like they were anaesthetised. At the same time she was wide awake and full of pointless anticipation. She looked at her less than perfect shape in a steamy mirror on the wall, and wondered that anyone should long for her. It was a mystery, but Joseph seemed to live in a world of pure emotion, like a faithful dog.

Later she remembered to look from her bedroom window, knowing that Joseph would also be gazing from his at the moon. He had said he would, and asked her to do the same, and that the light from their eyes would be reflected back to the moon and down to join them across the miles.

They had talked about love that night. When they were necking, she wanted to say she loved him, but instead it came out as, 'Do you love me?'

'Yes. I love you,' he said, but the way he said it only made her more anxious.

'But will you love me forever?'

'But do you love me?' was his response.

'Of course. You know I do,' she answered, thinking

anyway it was her Christian duty. 'But will you still love me when I'm old?'

'I love you now, isn't that what's important? How can I predict the future?' he asked, and elaborated on the subject till first she and then he lost track of his words.

II

'What's it like being married? Are you happy?'

'Oh yeah, very!' replied the cutter, with an open smile.

Joseph was giving him a lift home from work, on a high summer evening. The car windows were open and it would be light for hours to come.

'You have a child, haven't you?'

'Two,' said the cutter. 'Why, are you thinking of getting married?'

'As it happens… I've found someone,' Joseph said, dazed with love. 'I suppose you're not interested in other women anymore?'

'No. I love K.'

'Have you never been with anyone else then?'

'Not really. I went with some mates to London one time and visited a brasser in Soho. I didn't fancy it though.'

'Why's that?'

'Too much pressure, you know. She stripped off, and stood there in suspenders, lace and all, just what you want and all but whatever it was, I just couldn't get a bugle… It's nothing without love. So who is she, your love interest?'

'You don't know her,' said Joseph.

'I bet you can't wait between meetings to see her.'

'You're right about that.'

'So you wouldn't be interested in other women at this stage, either?'

'I'm not saying that.' He knew that if the opportunity arose, there was no line of resistance.

'That's terrible, Joey.'

'I know. I just can't help myself.'

III

It was another sunny morning. Deirdre's kid brother came to the door in his pyjamas when the doorbell rang.

On seeing Joseph, the kid brother instantly called out 'Aidan!'

'No,' said Joseph. 'It's Deirdre I'm here for.'

She came to the door and looked at him with her cheerful mock disdain.

'Let's go for a drive,' he said. He wanted to go somewhere with her and he thought of the Zoo.

'Shouldn't you be at work?' she asked, in the car.

'Has anybody ever asked you to marry them?' he asked, driving through the outskirts of town.

'I think so.'

'You think so – you mean you don't know?'

'It depends how you interpret the words… Is this a

proposal?'

'Yes.'

'I'm shocked!'

They travel in silence to the park. Joseph buys tickets and they squeeze through the black turnstile into the Zoo. There is nobody else around. The morning sun is hot on the grassy hillside where they sit down. At the same time chimpanzees are waking up and starting to move about on their island in the lake below them.

'So what do you think?' he asks.

'Oh Joseph, I hardly know you,' she says, '– and you don't really know me.'

'It's okay, you can say yes or no. I won't be upset.'

'Let me think about it,' she says.

'Great! So you will think about it?'

'Yes, I'll think about it.'

'Wow! How long?'

'Just give me a week,' she says, thinking she will put it to God at her weekly prayer meeting. More urgent than that, it would require in-depth woman-talk with Rosaleen.

In the event, God remained silent on the subject after she prayed over it, but Rosaleen had plenty to say. She paced up and down the kitchen like an interrogator, as Deirdre sat at the table sipping from a cup of coffee.

'Well if you don't want him, I'll take him,' Rosaleen said and laughed.

'You would too!'

'I would,' said Rosaleen, 'But it's not for marriage that

I'd want him!'

They both laughed.

'The problem is,' said Deirdre, 'he doesn't .. It's difficult to talk ..'

'C'mon – spit it out girl!'

'I can't.'

'What? He doesn't make love? What?'

'All he wants is to touch.'

'Ooh! Tell all…'

'I'm so frustrated. He only wants to touch, he never asks for more. I don't think he really loves me.'

'But you love him?'

'Yes, and he says he loves me – but I want him to prove it.'

'Tell him then.'

Frank came in from the pub one Sunday when Deirdre was alone in the kitchen, washing dishes. He said, 'I don't want to worry you, but you know Joseph is a bender.'

'What do you mean?' she asked.

'He's a woolly woofter.'

She laughed. 'Where did you get that idea! He's not!'

'That's what somebody in the pub said. How do you know he's not?'

She gave him a funny look.

'Trust me. We have ways,' she said.

'Somebody saw him coming out of that gay bar in town with another bloke.'

Deirdre laughed falteringly.

'No seriously,' Frank wheezed, laughing too. 'I swear to God.'

Joseph said, 'It just happened. I got drunk, and I didn't know what I was doing.'

'You mean to say you had sex with this person? Did you–'

'It was oral.'

'Oh my God! How could you do something like that? I'm not sure I can live with that!'

'It was a one-off. I don't know why it happened, and it is so disgusting and degrading.'

'I don't want to know! Any other secrets like that,' she said, 'I think you should just keep them to yourself from now on.'

'Ok,' he said.

She looked at him again and frowned. It seemed to her she ought to be more angry with him, but because he had been honest, she decided she would forgive him after about a week.

The next time when they parked up on a dark sideroad near the airport, after petting for a while she asked, 'What would you say if I asked you to make love to me now?'

'Well, eh, I guess we'd have to take precautions. You know.'

'Oh just let's go home!'

She never gave him his answer, but Joseph just sort of assumed they were engaged, and she played along with it. They looked in jewellery shop windows for engagement rings. She planned to design her own.

'Why do you keep sighing,' she asked him once, when they were sitting in her front parlour listening to records.

'I don't,' he said, but then sighed heavily again and realised. 'Oh! You're right. I don't know why.'

'You seem to be depressed.'

'No I'm not. I'm just a jolly, little man.'

'Joseph, you may be many things, but you are not a jolly little man!'

He sighed again and said, 'I wonder if I could get special dispensation from the Bishop to be married in a church, without actually saying the prayers?'

'But that is the most important part!'

'Well I don't believe in it.'

'Oh just forget it. I don't want to hear any more about it!'

She walked out and left him sitting on her sofa. He made his own way out. He could always switch between being with her or Aidan, so he was making himself quite at home in their house. Her father accepted Joseph, or rather ignored him, but her mother, who was small but formidable, was not at all impressed and avoided him.

'You can do a lot better than that,' she said. 'He's not of your same class, living in a Corporation house. He must be a gold-digger.'

'Oh mother, you're such a snob!' Deirdre said. 'You know what, don't talk about him anymore. We are in love!'

'You mark my words, he's not serious about you,' her mother said, but Deirdre ran to her room.

'And you're not serious about him!' her mother added.

IV

Summer was in its last blaze. It had been a perfect summer, in many ways, thanks to Joseph and something no other guys her age she knew had, the car. There was trail riding, in the Wicklow mountains, that day the horses took it into their heads to gallop. Other days too. The Furry Glen, down by the lily ponds, under the branches, and afterwards sprawling on a grassy bank, it was so heavenly. Stables there too, from where they went riding in the park. In many ways it was idyllic. There was a record they played called 'This is the Day' by Shusha, that told their best feelings.

Joseph seemed careless of her wants and he was thoughtless, that was it, thoughtless. He didn't like the cartoon sticker she wanted to put on the dashboard. A woman can't stay upset with a man who loves her, when they are twenty and deep in a hot summer that could have been made specially for them, but soon the summer would be ending.

Rosaleen continued to rib her about the lack of progress on the lovemaking front. Deirdre secretly felt it was worth hanging onto Joseph just to keep him out of Rosaleen's clutches. When Deirdre and Joseph were going to join Frank and his girlfriend for a weekend at Silverstrand. Rosaleen said if Joseph didn't go for it then, he never would.

They changed into swimsuits in the caravan on the first day at the seaside. Deirdre sat casually with her legs wide apart not a bit shy with Joseph, who looked her up and down. She wondered if he would ask about a small scar on her right calf, and she turned her leg in the hope that he would, but his eyes never got any lower than her bikini.

The caravan park was out of sight on the headland above the white, sandy beach. When they went down onto it there was nobody else there. After kicking a ball about for a while, they played jousting with Frank and Joseph as horses and Deirdre and Monica riders on their backs, trying to drag each other down laughing.

They were only staying the one night, Saturday, and going home on Sunday night because they all had to get back for work on Monday morning, except Deirdre. That night they drank whiskey and played strip poker in the caravan.

'The trouble is girls always chicken out when it gets interesting,' said Frank, dealing. 'The fellas will go on till the bitter end.'

Monica said that last year Frank had done a streak

around the caravan park in the middle of the night for a bet. As soon as the game got to a point where Monica would have had to lose her brassiere, the girls decided it was bedtime.

'See, didn't I tell you!' said Frank.

Monica and Frank tucked themselves away in what passed for a double bedroom in the caravan, leaving Deirdre alone with Joseph. According to Rosaleen's calculation this should have been their big moment, but Joseph was already falling asleep on the couch that served as his bed, so Deirdre left him there and retired to her own tiny room.

On Sunday there was a carnival in the town. Joseph announced that he was ill, and said he never went on those rides anyway – you had to be crazy. Deirdre felt let down and went ahead with Frank and Monica as Joseph watched from below.

On the night drive back to the city, Frank started singing *Working Class Hero*. He and Joseph were boisterous and laughing. The girls felt excluded. Joseph knew all the words to endless songs, everything from *Seven Drunken Nights* to *Like a Rolling Stone* and kept on singing for some time after the others had tired of it. By the time they hit the outskirts of the city even Joseph had gone quiet. It was pitch dark, with nothing to see but the headlights of other cars.

After dropping the other couple off at Monica's place, Joseph drove Deirdre home. It was shadowy under the tree outside her house where they pulled up.

She was still frustrated and jealous, though she knew it was silly, of how Frank and Joseph had left her out of the laughing, singing and talking on the way home. As usual they started kissing goodnight. She was wearing a light cotton dress, not her usual jeans, and when his hand slipped under, a sudden rage swelled in her and she jumped out of the car. She walked quickly to her door without saying anything. She was so furious she didn't want to speak.

'What's wrong?' he said, following her. 'Please tell me!'

She opened the door and just before going in she paused.

'If you don't know, I can't tell you,' she said.

He was dumbstruck.

'You've even put me off sex,' she said, and shut the door on him.

V

Aidan is putting a small suitcase into the back of Joseph's car. There are so many of Aidan's siblings that they have to take it in turns to share the cottage their parents always rent for the summer holidays. Now he and Joseph are driving there to join them. It's almost as if Joseph is one of the family.

'How many miles is it to Achill? About three hundred, I suppose,' says Joseph. 'Let's see if we could average sixty miles an hour, it would take 5 hours. But then, there's traffic...'

'Remember, Joseph, it's not getting there that's important, it's the journey. Take it easy! We can drive fifty or sixty miles, then stop for a pint. There's no hurry.'

'I haven't seen Deirdre for two weeks now. How long have they been there already?'

'One week.'

'She wouldn't see me you know. I'll try to patch things up with her.'

Aidan hardly listens as Joseph continues to rabbit, on the drive westward. They play tapes on the stereo. *Tell Me That It Isn't True*. Aidan has never known such a neurotic with such a lot of ideas of so little use, flitting from theory to theory with seldom a pause. Joseph's lack of self-awareness allows Aidan a sort of comfortable invisibility, which he values more than anything.

They make two stops on the way. The second one is not far from their destination on the remote West coast. Aidan and Joseph buy pints of ale in a large empty lounge, where signed pictures of Robert Shaw hang on the wall. Carrying their drinks outside, they walk around the building and down a lane lined with fuchsia in bloom. They are talking about Deirdre again.

'Don't worry about it Joseph. She always does this. I've lost count of the number of times.'

'What do you mean don't worry? I'm engaged to her.'

'Have you told anybody?'

'No.'

'If you haven't told anybody,' says Aidan, 'you're not engaged.'

As they round the back of the building a panorama opens up across cliffs and over the bay with many islands. They sit at a table by the cliff-top balustrade. Aidan points to the distance and says, 'That's where we're going. That's Achill.'

'That's where she is,' says Joseph.

Aidan quaffs some beer and says, 'You've got to be prepared for something Joe. There's someone else.'

'What do you mean?'

'She's met someone there.'

The last stretch of the journey takes them across Achill sound. After the last shop with its ancient red petrol pumps, a straight single track runs through brackish bogland. The road is lined with yellow gorse. On one side, rocks lead down to a seven-mile beach. In front of them, a heather blue mountain has its head in a liquid white cloud.

'What's his name?'

'Rusty. We met him the last time the family came here.'

'What is he?' asks Joseph, as they approach a humpback bridge, where a torrent of bronze water flows from the mountain.

'Don't worry he's not a patch on you. I think he's an artificial inseminator,' he lies.

Joseph's concentration lapses and the car bumps

roughly over the humpback bridge.

'I'll kill him.'

'No you won't!' says Aidan.

When they reach the rented whitewashed cottage, Aidan leads the way and they put their luggage into one of the bedrooms. They are used to travelling around the coast, and sharing guest house bedrooms like brothers. Aidan's brother Frank, is inside listening to Suffragette City and practicing on his guitar. The LP cover lies on one of the beds: *Ziggy Stardust*. When they come in he turns off the record player.

'Hello Joe,' he says without looking up.

The thought passes between the three that there will soon be an awkward meeting. Joseph drops his holdall in the bedroom and goes back out. When he does, Deirdre is standing there. Frank starts singing in the bedroom, '*We told her she was beautiful / We told her she was free / But none of us would meet her / In the house of mystery.*'

'Can I talk to you?'

'We can go for a walk,' she says.

They walk down a stony lane and onto the road out of the village below. She reaches over and holds his hand on the way. His heart soars.

'Can we patch things up?' he asks.

'It's too late,' she says.

They sit on an isolated bench above a rocky beach. To the west the sea is crashing onto the corner of high cliffs.

'Is there nothing I can do then?' he asks.

'I'm sorry Joe. It's over,' she says.

He covers his eyes.

'I have to go now,' she says. 'We're going out sea fishing…Do you want to come? Last time we caught a conger eel!'

'It's okay. You know me, I'd only be seasick.'

Deirdre walks back to the village. He sits there for a long time. After a while he sees the tiny rowing boat far out on the ocean, where she is braving waves and sea monsters.

Novices and Pros

I

The monkey-suited bouncer in the doorway at Zhivago's Night Club just shook his head. Joseph turned and made his way towards a bar further down the block. It was October and the evening was damp with mist. He sat at the bar drinking vodka and lime, hoping for a chance encounter. All he met were the backs and shoulders of conventionally dressed people shoving their way to the bar to order. There was no big-hipped Venus looking for action, no charming phrases exchanged with intelligent and sultry girls bored with office work. He stayed till he began to feel out of place and then continued to the next pub, and another pair of vodkas.

He had money to spend, since starting work in the warehouse. The packed bar of O'Donoghue's was his second stop. His boots and clothing felt looser than they used to, which made him feel self-consciously dowdy. He swallowed more vodkas. There was no chance of talking to anybody where he sat at the bar. A well-known woman journalist (who started off as a flaming Marxist and ended up a holy humbug) was talking to a beautiful girl with waist-length, red hair. People were standing in circles and milling around him.

He stepped back into the night air and drifted as far as the Baggot Inn, on the next corner. Upstairs a band called U2 was hammering out enough energy to drain the national grid.

If you walk away, walk away, walk away
I will follow, I will follow

In the damp, dark bar downstairs he put away a double whiskey and ginger ale, while the bass thudded overhead.

Falling into it again, low-rise buildings sheltered the narrow street. Couples were linking, laughing and jostling. As far as Mercer Street he strayed, and there found himself in front of an ornate pub. Outside a father argues with a barman who, blocking his way with calming gesture responds. The father shouts 'I want him out of there. He's my son!'

'Be reasonable,' the barman seems to say, 'he– '

This must be a gay bar. One more pub, one more drink, what harm could it do. Joseph goes through the doors and leaves the arguers outside. He's thinking he'll order a bloody Mary, for the occasion. At least it's not crowded like the other pubs. The Carpenters are piping.

I'm on the top of the world
Looking down on creation.

Climb to the red plush barstool, and another drink. The barman is fielding a lame joke from one of the customers, something about hot toddy 'on the rocks.' A stocky fellow moves to the next barstool and says something to Joseph in a mild rural accent.

'What do you think about the place?'

'Surprising,' Joseph says, leaning on the bar. 'I thought it would be all men.'

'That's what I used to think. You have to look closely at some of them,' says the other fellow. He is round-faced, and wearing a black cashmere overcoat. They tell their names; the other one is called Martin Pender. He ventures, 'You're in no condition to go home yet,' when Joseph gets up clumsily to leave. Pender follows and offers a lift, but first to his flat for a coffee and to sober up.

The car is now heading up Amiens Street, past White Friars Church into bedsit land, somewhere in Harold's Cross. Joseph, sitting back, hears without listening Joe Dolan on the stereo singing:

I'm in love with the girl who lives
In the house with the whitewashed gable

What would it be like to be a fabulous pop star, who in a car crash lost his balls, then singing castrato like that? How you would glow, martyr with a voice like an angel, singing of heartbreak till they thought they were in Heaven listening, and all the standing ovations they would give and encores they would clamour for. Nobody could ever sing as high as you. 'He lost his balls you know, in a car crash,' they would say. 'He's thinking of running for Prime Minister.'

Joseph remembered nothing till he was naked on the coverlet of a single bed in a small room. He tried to talk while Pender, also naked, sixty-nined him. Pender's stiff little prick was in front of his face.

'I'm training to be a priest,' Pender answers Joseph's question. 'But I'm giving it up.'

'Why's that?' Joseph interrupts Pender's sucking again.

'I got disillusioned with the seminary. The fellows there are not interested in Religion. All they want is to do this every night.'

Joseph was drifting in and out of his senses. He could feel nothing. Pender was saying, 'I'll mop that up,' and wiping semen from the coverlet with a towel. It was a white towel like you get in hotels. Joseph put on his pants, then stood over the corner sink and violently puked. He was not exactly clear what had just happened, but he was racked with waves of apprehension. With each wave more, the more he vomited.

When he stopped puking, and rinsed the sink a little, Pender drove him home. The roads were empty under the streetlights. As they swung down by the concrete flats, Joseph indicated to Pender to stop a block away from where he lived, then got out and walked. Pender followed him to his door, and asked about seeing him again. Joseph tried to get out of it with a noncommittal answer but Pender turned up at his door a few weeks later. Joseph went and talked to him in the same way as he would have to a door-to-door salesman. No, was the answer, and no not another time.

Joseph's mother said, 'Why didn't you ask your friend to come in?'

'He's not my friend.'

'Who was he? What did he want?'

'Look, just forget it! He's nobody.'

II

'My God, I thought I saw some filthy toilets in Bombay, but this is the worst I have ever seen!' said the Indian businessman, flicking water from his hands as he stepped out into the warehouse yard. There were articulated lorries and forty-foot containers all around. One of them was unloading cheesecloth from India, and Joseph was piling it onto wooden pallets for the diesel forklift to take inside. The warehouse was a cold, high-ceilinged hall, rank with diesel smoke and, in the morning, giant guard-dog turds.

In one section a warehouseman was singing 'Sixteen Tons' in falsetto. Cecil, the toothless Bond clerk shuffled by in his biscuit brown workcoat. Vinny the forklift driver, a swarthy joker in his fifties, ribbed him, 'Well Cecil, did she do the bold thing last night?' Vinny sucked the last smoke from a quarter-inch coffin-nailer that he held pinched between thumbnail and forefinger before flicking it away.

'No, we stopped all that a long time ago,' said the Bond clerk.

'How about you, Joey, did you bury the baldy fella last night?' asked Vinny, sitting in the forklift truck in a heavy donkey jacket while Joseph, in tee-shirt and jeans, loaded the pallet.

'As Stavros's wife said,' quipped Joseph. '– Stavros, Kojak, baldy fella – get it?' It was his way of avoiding the question.

'Har-de-har-har,' said Vinny. 'You're so sharp you'll cut yourself.'

'He has no girlfriend,' said the Gaffer, a bony sour-faced man who managed the warehouse.

'That's no problem – sure he could always find one down on Haddington Road,' said Vinny.

'Will yez come on – tea's up!' wheezed a plump red-faced worker standing in the doorway of the hut where they took their breaks. When the Gaffer walked past the door of the hut out into the street, the plump worker sang in a whisper, 'Here's the robbers passing by.'

Vinny shook his head. 'That's terrible. It's loose talk like that that costs jobs.'

As Joseph drove into town that Friday night, with a small share of his pay packet still on him after paying for his keep, their words swirled around in his head.

'Did you bury the baldy fella?' 'He has no girl…' 'Haddington Road…' He had just bought an old Prinz car for sixty pounds, with a knot tied in the accelerator cable.

The streetwalkers were on Haddington Road, standing near corners and at the end of one of the canal bridges. Joseph parked the car in a nearby street, and walked back to where he had seen them. It was a winter night with no sky, only a dark absence beyond the streetlamps. Wet branches of trees circled the lights in droplets. The black canal separated two streets where high-stepped terraces of grand houses leaned back, behind their railed gardens. He could see his breath. A couple of brassers were slagging off some old geezer, who came just to look or vice versa. One of them approached Joseph.

'Are you looking for business, love?'

In a minute he was down a dark alley with her up against a wall. She hoisted her skirts and tried to let him have his way with her there in the open air. Nobody was around but the corner of the street was still in view. It was cold and nothing happened. He paid her anyway, and walked away.

Most days he managed the storeroom and lugged fabric. The factory was separate from the warehouse, in a cobbled street near the cattle market. The work was heavy, but not too much for a fit twenty-one-year-old. After a hard day unloading tons of denim from forty-foot containers, he would feel only a pleasing weariness that enhanced the pleasure of sleep.

There never seemed to be any room left in the building to store the latest consignments. Often the delivery men would just pile stuff in the street, leaving Joseph and his helpers to find a place for it. They wrapped Sellotape halfway around old cutting machine blades and used them to cut the baling tape on boxes. Then they strapped the bolts of cloth to an electric hoist and raised them to the first floor.

Joseph never let up, always in and out of containers carrying bales, running down stairs, recording details. The helpers were more interested in talking about pigeon lofts, and getting the most out of their cigarette breaks. They called each other 'Cunt,' 'Prick' and 'Bollix' interchangeably. They would look at Joseph sweating over the work while they sat next to him on a bale, smoking, and smile at each other.

'Here Prick, what do you think of Joey?'

'He's all right I suppose, Cunt.'

'Yeah, he's not so bad, Bollix.'

'If you like gick.' They laughed.

When the boss pressed him about finishing the work, Joseph was on the point of breakdown.

'I'm not cut out for this. I don't know if I can do this.'

'Take it easy,' said the boss. 'Don't let them get to you.' And then he said something that Joseph could never understand, 'You're a good worker, it's just that you have a small flaw in your personality.'

There was a milkwater moon over the canal at Haddington Road. On the spit-blackened bridge another woman was waiting. This one had a teenage girl with her. They led him down steps into a dark basement garden. It was not clear which one he would get. The big woman undid herself and him. They were hidden from view but the footpath was just above them. She told the girl to let him put his hand down her pants at the same time, but even then it didn't work.

The next time Joseph thought he would kerb-crawl in the car like other drivers he'd seen. A good-looking girl approached when he slowed near her. He stopped and wound down the passenger-side window. She leaned in and spoke with an English accent.

'It's five pounds for a hand job, ten pounds to suck you off, and twenty pounds for full sex.'

He let her in and she told him to drive across the bridge, back towards Baggot Street. Turn into a small alley on the left.

'What is your name?'

'Louise.'

'My name is Joseph.'

Something about her accent and where she was from. He felt at ease, and she was too. He thought it was like being on a blind date. She told him where to park in the back alley behind a mews, and led him through a tall gate into a walled yard. He followed her into the ground-floor flat. It was hot from a three-bar electric fire that was left on. She turned and stood in the bedroom door.

'The bathroom is through there, if you want to wash first,' she said, pointing around to her right.

'It's okay. I had a bath before I came out.'

It was a small bedroom with red curtains. There was a chair at the foot of the bed, and a chiffonier at the head. That was where Louise was standing when she released her breasts. Joseph had already placed everything but his shirt on the chair.

'You're not shy, are you,' she said, as he took off his shirt.

'It's not something I've ever suffered from,' he said.

They were both naked then and Louise lay back on the bed, revealing just a line between her legs. Joseph said, 'I'm really nervous. This is my first time – well first proper time.'

'You'll be fine,' she said, and toyed with him till he got hard. Then she placed a condom on him. He mounted her, and it only took a minute or two of penetration and infantile drooling on her shoulder till he came. She lay back and rested, feeling as safe as if she were invisible.

'Thank God,' he said. 'I thought I could never do it.'

'Why is that?'

He explained to her about the street and the other women. That was understandable, she said. They talked for a while. She stayed lying on the bed, when he got up and dressed. He put his money on the chiffonier, and left her an extra tenner.

'How will I find you again?'

'Just drive around,' she said.

He drove and drove, but he never found Louise again.

New Year's Eve

Joseph sat in the corner of the sofa, full of teenage apprehension that soon his mother would force him to join in the usual 'one big happy family' act. At midnight, she would drag him up, embarrassingly joining hands with his father. Next it would be 'Should old acquaintance be forgot' with the arms up and down and all the rest. Then, compulsory for Joseph, ritual pronunciation of 'happy new year' in a voice thick with reluctance and misanthropy.

On The Late Late Show a man was telling anecdotes about Dublin in the old days, when people used to get presents of things they would need for death, and how most people to this day still kept a blessed candle in the house. Over the back of the light armchair into which he had just flopped, his father mumbled, 'He's a bullshitter.' He had his reasons for saying it, but he wasn't sharing them.

Joseph wavered deep in contempt for a second but then said, 'Well, so are you.' It was the first time he had ever criticised his father, aloud. Without turning to Joseph or in any way arguing his case his father said, 'I know I am.' Christ, thought Joseph, that's how they dribble a vast web of guilt over everything and everyone, making you see yourself, reflecting your own crass nothingness, your own most contemptible failings incarnate, endless, unstill, infuriating.

Deliver us also from the Change of Life, Joseph thought. His mother like all the women of her age 'suffered with her nerves.' She was working in the kitchen with tears on her face when Joseph went in to collect a cup of tea. He thought it was that she had heard what he said to his father.

These showcase occasions of hers were always shattered by Joseph's violent reaction against them. At Christmas she had broken down over some remark he had made at the dinner table. Such was the tradition. It was almost the only time they ever had to sit together at one table. The feeling that it was all a fraud with them, all phoney, tormented Joseph. Yet he was forced to conform to their rituals on pain of whingeing, spite and verbal assault from his mother, inducing tidal waves of anguish in him for being responsible yet too weak to change anything.

Joseph was peeling hot fat from ham just out of the pressure cooker, when at the stroke of midnight according to the Late Late Show, his mother and kid sister went outside to listen for the peal of bells from Christ's Church.

'Ah, can't hear them,' his mother said, outside. 'The wind is blowing the wrong way. Very faint...'

'I can hear them,' his kid sister said, 'Or maybe it's the television.'

Joseph retreated back into his corner of the sofa, behind the back of his father's chair. His mother came over, her face covered in tears, and she reached down to him. Joseph was worried about her. She clutched his hand feebly, like a person drowning.

'They ought to be here with us,' she cried.

It dawned on Joseph that the reason why his mother had broken down again was nothing to do with what he had said to his father. His newlywed sister was out in the wilds of Kildare in her purchase house, without transport. His dancing sister was down the road in a church hall. His father did not cease to watch TV.

'They'll all be here tomorrow,' Joseph reminded her.

Her face was one of total grief, moving and appalling to him. She also seemed to express her hope for him, but he was paralysed, powerless to express his own furious misery.

'Try not to use every occasion as an excuse for crying,' Joseph said, in desperation – it was the only thing he could think of. He feared for her heart. Maybe if she could struggle on for a year or two through the Change, she would be in the clear. But he did not have faith his mother could last that long, the way she was burning herself out. She went upstairs.

Now The Cop Cats came on TV, a choir of men in

stupid-looking kilts. Joseph said, 'They're all cops.' It was a sort of peace offering to his father who was trying to climb out of his chair.

'Irish?'

'Yeah.'

They were singing 'May each day of your life be a good day.'

'I'm off,' his father puffed, 'Goodnight Joseph!'

'See you, goodnight.'

Now he could switch over to BBC2 where the rock highlights of the year were on. He would have to shift his kid sister, who had reappeared.

'C'mon, off you go... Say goodnight to Mammy when you go up.'

His mother came back down, looking for her tranquillisers. She was quiet. Joseph went into the kitchen with her.

'Well, what did you get up to tonight?' he asked.

'Oh, I had a most depressing night.'

'What happened?

'Well first me and Kay went up to Bee Murphy's. Bee had invited us up — just for an hour like — to talk to George.'

'Oh, is he home?'

'Yes, they sent him home. They said there's nothing more they can do for him, that he might as well be at home... And he's very, very sick. He frightened the life out of us,' she said in a tone of immense concern. 'Then later on we go over to the pub for a while. And your father wouldn't bother so much as to turn his head to look at us when we came in. With his crowd of drunken oul'fellas who couldn't even stand up. And I'm not joking you, every one of them in that place was paralytic – out of their minds.'

Joseph's dancing sister came in then, and to make up to his mother for the dull New Year's Eve, he put on a bit of an act with 'Happy new year!' and swinging his dancing sister around, and giving her a half-hearted peck on the cheek.

'What's wrong?' his sister said, on seeing their mother.

'You weren't here at midnight Cinderella,' Joseph said.

'I never even thought of it,' she said.

Their mother said she had thought of driving out to Kildare to the newlywed sister and spouse to rescue them from 'sitting looking at each other.'

'But they're out there every night!' Joseph said.

'Yes,' his mother said, her voice thickening. 'But it's the time of year. Out there with a crowd of strangers. But no, Your Father said that was just my interfering. Could I not just leave them alone – they probably prefer that. Well maybe they do, but how do we know that?'

She paused for a moment and then said, reflectively, 'Some people can be so callous.'

This talk was going to go on for a long time. Joseph was not relishing having to form opinions on these things.

'I'll tell you what I would like to do,' she said, with new enthusiasm, 'is to help old folks, left alone, away from their families.'

'Well why don't you? You could join The Legion of Mary or something,' he said.

'What the hell good is that, stuck in praying, six days out of seven.'

'Not necessarily them, just some...'

'Aren't people very callous? Now there's George: three weeks ago he was out at parties living it up with us and now he's sitting at home, at death's door. Yet when we go over to his friends in the pub, the very same grotty old drunkenness goes on.'

'This is it.'

Joseph sighed. He was well and truly fed up being distracted from Rock Highlights of the Year. His dancing sister cannily retired to bed and leaving him to the conversation.

'Now take your father, for instance. Although he comes home with the money every weekend and has always done his duty by us – and I mean you've got to hand it to him – inside there's nothing. He has no heart.'

Joseph resented these recriminations, especially since he was feeling more callous than most. He kept wanting to say 'Stop poisoning our minds.' She never shut up complaining about his father in endless obsession, betraying her own desire, trying to win the children over. But Joseph was too wound-up to speak, too tormented by conflicting thoughts to frame a meaningful utterance, although his mother seemed to think both of them were exercising free speech.

'And Kay's husband is just the same, basically. He does take her out the odd time. Like recently they went to Paris for a weekend – he has the money, you see. But deep down he's as cold and callous... His father is living with his sister's family and the poor man is eighty and completely deaf. They're out early in the morning while he lies upstairs all day till they come back from work. He can't even hear a knock on the door. But what can you do? Their whole family's attitude is that because he's eighty his time has come and that's that. If you try to help, it's just interference.'

'Now look!' Joseph explained, 'You've got your lines crossed somewhere. You're only worrying about what you can do nothing about. And yet you don't bother helping anywhere you could. You're miserable over-'

'No I'm not miserable,' she cried, 'I'm happy in my own life.'

'For God's sake, you're saying the exact opposite of the truth. You're going to have to face up to things as they really are. You're doing everybody else's suffering as if you hadn't enough of your own.'

'I'm not crying for myself. I'm not! I'm crying for the way people are. Admittedly I do cry a lot. Ever since I was a child I've been very bad for crying... My bladder is near my eyes.'

He knew she was going to say that.

'But then again, for a few months after I came out of hospital I couldn't cry at all, even when people died, I had realised how few people cared about me one way or the other. When people had crowds of visitors, your father thought hard of coming in. And when he did, he just sat there without saying a word. Do you realise that to this day that man doesn't even know what operation I had or what the reason was for me passing out? He never so much as asked the doctors how I was doing. And yet I know that if he took bad tomorrow, I would be up in that hospital every other hour, looking after him. I was crying for the way people are. It must he great not to care. It must he great! But you have to be born that way.'

'Yes it is great. It's great!' Joseph said, as if attacked, 'We think about the same things but they don't have the same effect on us. Take me: all that worries me is work and entertainment. Frankly I couldn't give a damn about George's cancer. I don't know George. I'm not going to do anything about any of these things. It's as simple as that. *I'm not going to do anything about them!* I know that for a fact. And whatever use it might be to worry about things I'm going to do, it's absolutely pointless to worry about things I don't know and never will.'

'Ok,' his mother answered, now with something to defend, 'But if Kay came to that door in the middle of the night and said that their car was broken down and their daughter was sick would you please give her a lift to the hospital, what would you say?'

'Yes.'

'And would you mind?'

'No.'

'No, nor would I. But Your Father would! I wasn't fretting about that old man, I was just using an example of how callous some people are.'

There was a weird and ugly cartoon on the TV.

'What the hell is that?' his mother asked.

'Don't know, I often wonder where they get those. They look old, but I don't think they are. They're all junkies you know.'

'That's just what it looks like, something a mad mind would think up. Like, there were youngfellas in the pub tonight and one of them had a mask. It was the weirdest thing you ever saw. It wasn't of a monkey or anything – it was a mask of a very, very old man. They were standing in the doorway when we arrived. Well! Do you think we could get Kay to go in! We told her it was only a youngfella with a mask, pretending to be drunk. But no, all she kept saying was it was an old man like her father-in-law that couldn't stand up – and they were carrying him out.'

The Hat

His mother's black felt hat with the wide brim did not actually blow away, but it was left on the back of a pickup truck one cold night. Joseph, Aidan and Jim had hitched a lift outside a pub in Wicklow, south towards Waterford. They had set out from Dublin that Thursday morning to hitchhike to a monastery in Tipperary where Jim's uncle was a monk. There was only room for one in the cab with the driver, so Aidan and Joseph sat in the open back of the pickup with some big paint tins. They pulled a tarpaulin up over their legs against the cold wind, and under there was where the hat was left to stop it from blowing away.

Later that night they stepped out of another pub on the quays in Waterford, after closing time. Jim said he knew somebody who worked night shift at a bakery in the town, so they followed him away from the quays through the wide, empty night streets. It was after midnight and the only people they saw were water inspectors, listening for leaks with long metal tubes from their ears to the ground.

They sat down by a wall in the backyard of the bakery, and wrapped their coats as tight to their necks as they could. Joseph only had an army surplus jacket and red corduroy jeans. Jim had a duffle coat with a hood, and Aidan had a long, black loden coat. The full moon was on their left in a cloudless sky when they sat down on the ground. There was only one window lit faintly on the third floor of the building. By the time their contact showed, the moon had moved to right of centre in the black sky. They were half-expecting either food or shelter from the bakery, but the contact offered nothing only directions to somewhere he said they could sleep.

The place was on the road out of town going towards Dungarvan. It was the derelict wreck of a huge building bombarded during the Civil War. They walked in the dark through its roofless shell, where the ground was strewn with rubble and overgrown with nettles and weeds. It was open to the sky and had an ominous atmosphere in the shadows of its broken walls. Picking their way through the ruins they saw nowhere to lie down, let alone sleep, so they agreed to find their way out and try and hitch a lift to Cork.

They thumbed for a while beside a junction. Bloated rats were swarming over some rubbish behind a billboard. Aidan said, 'We might as well walk.'

Outside of town there was a clean industrial estate, opposite a few semi-detached houses. They shivered the rest of the night in the doorway of one of the industrial units. The others slept, but Joseph was too cold and his eyes never closed for long before opening again. About dawn, a security man on his rounds in a marked Ford Escort van pulled up across the road and made to get out. He didn't have to say anything, they hoisted their aching bones and left.

It turned into a hot sunny day on the road to Cork. They found themselves in wilderness with overgrown verges by the roadside. The others went and crapped in the ferns, but that was something inconceivable for Joseph who could not even pee at a public urinal.

A blonde Swedish tourist, not much older than them, gave them a lift in his hire car over the winding mountain road. He was playing a Canned Heat tape on the car stereo and swigging Coca Cola as they swung through hairpin bends, above steep cliff sides and valleys far into the distance below.

Well I'm so tired of cryin'
But I'm out on the road again
I'm on the road again

In Cork they had a mixed grill with button mushrooms and the works, in a Wimpy bar with the young Swede. Outside a man walked with a red flag in front of a train that was crossing a street from the docks. They climbed a steep hill with a church at the top and started hitch-hiking again. A helldriver stopped and took them bouncing and speeding in a low-ceilinged Ford Capri to a small town in Tipperary.

Aidan and Joseph were going to buy some biscuits in a shop down a few steps from the square in the town, while Jim was on the phone to his uncle.

'No, no it's not necessary,' Jim said, beckoning them out. They waited by a sunny stone wall near a Y junction at the top of the town. In about fifteen minutes, Jim's uncle Finbar, the monk, pulled up in a small car and drove them to the monastery.

On its own hillside with extensive grounds, the big stone building had a wide gravel driveway with a fountain in the middle. There were farm outhouses on one side, and everything needed for a farm that kept the monks self-sufficient. It was not possible for Joseph to view the place without remembering St Benedict's motto, which the Brothers had repeated to them so often, 'To work is to pray.'

An oak staircase led from the high-ceilinged entrance hall to the corridor and the room with bunk beds where they were to stay for Friday and Saturday nights. The monastery was open to anyone who wanted to stay and heal their souls, be fed and housed, all for free or an optional offering when you left. Jim had a guitar with him and Finbar the monk visited their room, sat on a chair in the middle and accompanied himself in a Gregorian version of

Suzanne takes you down
To her place by the river...
(It was no longer a silent order.)

A walk in the grounds and they looked in on a steaming, stamping bull, giant in its stall, with balls the size of mangoes. The day was whiled away playing ping pong in the clubhouse across the gravel driveway, past the sprinkling fountain. There were four bunk beds in their room, two up and two down. They slept in their underpants, Joseph in a top bunk, the others below. Jim said he would wake them at five in the morning to go see the monks sing matins in the chapel, but they slept right through.

Breakfast was cornflakes, farm milk, homemade bread and tea on solid wooden tables in the dining room. For dinner the monks served their guests small portions of boiled vegetables and meat from the farm. Of the few guests, there were some who would definitely leave an optional payment when they went; but Joseph, Aidan and Jim were not among them. There was little left from the five pounds or so that each had started out with.

On Saturday morning in the roomy, solid old bathroom, Joseph succeeded in expelling a painful three-day turd, since when nothing could trouble him. After some barren hitch-hiking on Sunday, having left in time to avoid Mass, they reached Mallow at nightfall. It was only a small town with a few terraces of whitewashed cottages, and one main road.

The railway station was open, and there was no one around, so they slept on the narrow wooden benches around the walls of the waiting room. It was warm enough but there was continual loud noise all night from trains shunting and passing through. They were lucky next day and got a lift all the way to the high seawalls of Bray. From there, they had enough coins to catch buses the rest of the way.

Some days after Joseph got home, his mother asked if anyone knew where her black funeral hat had got to. Joseph thought for a moment. It was only then he remembered placing the hat under the tarpaulin.

'It blew away,' he said.

The Green

Bicycle Days

The morning sun shines in. Joseph slots his jeans and tee-shirt on, draws the yellow curtains, and swoops down the stairs. It is the summer of being sixteen. In the kitchen his father is hunched over the table with a cup of tea. The kitchen blinds are down and the light is on. Joseph opens the blinds and turns off the light. He puts some corn flakes in a bowl, sloshes some milk in and wolfs them down.

His two friends from the Green are outside, he sees them stopping outside the gate, leaning over on their bikes. The Corporation estate houses are on their way going towards the seaside. Joseph grabs a towel and as he goes, his father closes the blinds, turns on the light and hunches over the cup of tea again. Joseph gets the old black bike from the shed, swings the garden gate and rides off, sitting upright with his hands down by his side.

The smell of tarmac is rising everywhere, sizzling

under the sun, as the three of them are cycling to the beach. Rolled-up towels are warming on the carriers of their bikes. Beyond the end walls of the purchase houses, tinker caravans and horses shimmer across a roadside field. Joseph's front wheel has a slow puncture, and the friends stop ahead while he pumps it up yet again. From caravans nearby, a man saunters over, in dusty clothes.

'Here, let me have a look.'

He produces a jemmy and prises out the inner tube.

'Ye haven't got an ould cigarette, have ye?' he asks.

Joseph gives him down a cigarette and a light. The man continues testing for leaks by spitting on his finger and touching the tube here and there. The spit fizzles at the side of an old puncture repair patch. The man pulls out his shirt, tears a strip off the inner seam, and ties it around the tube where it's patched. Amazingly, it works.

Just a few more miles by concrete roads, wheeling past quiet local shops and houses, with strips of grass and shady trees between the street and the footpath. Still no glimpse of the sea when they turn at a small sign pointing the way down a lane to the beach.

Where the lane runs out, they trudge, bikes and all, over white sand and marram grass. In a hollow on one side, a couple are making love under a bomber jacket. Beyond the high dunes, the tide is in. Rolling breakers stretch for miles in the sea-swept breeze.

Leave clothes here. The wet sand oozes between his

toes. There are a few people swimming, in the distance. Couples leap, splashing water on each other. Sometimes Joseph's feet slither on bladderwrack, sometimes they stub on hard stone. Remember to swim parallel to the shore. Try floating awhile. Then run out through the lukewarm shallows. The salt stings his sinuses when he lies back, letting the sun dry him, all goosebumps in the gritty sand.

Night. Close the yellow curtains. Hit the pillow, still hearing the sea in a shell. Feel the waves, lifting, falling, lifting, floating, again, and again – forever.

A Summer Job

This lunchtime the guys had a golden knife they were throwing at a wooden crate in the storeroom. It was a throwing knife with a diamond-shaped blade, designed so that no matter how badly you threw it, the point would always lead the way. It belonged to Ernie, the delivery driver.

When Ernie and the other guys left, they let Joseph mind the knife. Joseph had taken this summer job with the billposters, for a few weeks before he was meant to go back to school. He was throwing the knife, ineffectually, when the girl from the office came in looking for something. 'Has anyone seen Ernie,' she asked, though there was nobody else there. Her name was Nuala. She was stocky, so her short A-line dress had plenty to uncover when she moved and it didn't.

'They just left,' Joseph said, retrieving the knife from the floor by the crate. She watched as he threw it again. Once again it failed to stick in the wood.

'That looks cool. Can I try?'

Joseph let her get the knife, and half sat on a crate to watch her, doubled forward. Nuala threw the knife, and it flopped onto the floor. The square cut neck of her dress bowed as she picked it up. On her next throw the knife flew and stuck fast in the rough wood.

'Your turn now.' He didn't move. 'Well get it,' she said.

'I don't want to.'

'I thought it might be something like that,' she said, hesitating and giving him a long look before leaving.

He went back to the despatch room. This was his area, the place where he prepared the posters. The sliding door was always open onto the yard outside where the company had its own diesel pump.

Beyond the yard was a backroad along the south bank of the Poddle, a small tributary of the Liffey, near Kilmainham. On the other side of the river, the bank rose steeply to back gardens that were about a half a mile from the billposters' yard, and perhaps the equivalent of eight stories higher.

There was a woman settling on a lounger in a garden all that distance away on the far bank. Joseph stepped into the doorway in the bright summer air. The woman was wearing some sort of a sarong, and as he looked up she crossed or uncrossed her legs, and he thought their eyes connected. Can you make eye contact across a half a mile, he wondered? She was only the size of the top half of his thumb. He hoped she would be there every afternoon.

There was time for this after the morning's posters had all gone out and there was no rush to prepare tomorrow's. He refrained from looking at the woman and turned to preparing posters. He took the numbered panels and wet them in a trough of water on the purpose-built table, then rolled them up and placed them on slatted wooden shelves, ready to go out.

Close up, the dots that made up the pictures were the size of small coins. It was not obvious what the final picture would be when assembled and viewed from a distance. They were mostly tobacco posters – Carrolls, Players Number Six, Golden Virginia – and the occasional movie one. Today it was The Happy Hooker.

The evening turned overcast as the white pickup van bowled along with three in the front seat, Joseph in the middle. The middle-aged billposter picked up a porno magazine that was lying on a shelf under the glove compartment. Ernie the driver wore tight jeans and a permanent grin.

It was a difficult site in a strange part of the city, a dull square. Joseph blocked one lane of the traffic coming round a corner, while the billposter went up triple-high ladders, like a circus trapeze man. Joseph could see the panels were too wet, and he felt guilty as he watched the billposter peel them painstakingly off the roll, to paste The Happy Hooker high above the intersection.

Student Exchanges

The Green was the centre of everything that summer, when Joseph turned sixteen and decided he didn't want to go back to school. In a circular cul-de-sac, it was worn dusty in the middle from football. Like every green in the whole jerry-built town, it had a crooked sapling stuck at one end. Joseph used to pass by there on his way to the filthy system-built Corporation estate to the north. He met up with boys from the Green in the hayfields on the borderline of the estate, when they challenged the estate kids to a game of football.

He had to walk past the Green on his way home from school. It happened sometimes that Matthew from the Green was walking home at the same time and they walked together.

'Have you ever done anything really bad?' Matthew asked.

'I don't think so. Like what?'

'I have. I strangled a cat.'

Joseph said he had seen a headless puppy dumped on waste ground.

'I don't know what sort of person could do that. They're hardly human,' he said.

Matthew said that people threw darts and fired airguns at cats who came into their gardens. They stopped into Matthew's house near the Berlin wall into the Corporation estate. Matthew lent Joseph Rubber Soul. They exchanged records on loan, till Joseph's mother asked him to hand Matthew's parents a note in an envelope, and when he did they gave him a five pound note.

Joseph's mother said, 'Thanks be to God. It's just to tide us over.'

He gave them back the five pounds after a few days. Joseph noticed Matthew putting his records upstairs when he came to the door.

Whenever there was a 'free house' – no parents – the word went out and an ad hoc party was held. One night, it happened to be in the house of a family of sisters like every neighbourhood has – all gorgeous, one stratospherically remote and beautiful. All the rooms were darkened, and 'Je t'aime' was playing in the parlour. There were people everywhere. Joseph went up the dimly lit stairs, looking for Maura, and found her in one of the bedrooms, necking with another guy.

Maybe the heart needs to be broken, for reasons unknown. Joseph had fallen for Maura more or less on the basis of one friendly conversation, alone together at the corner by the Green, as winter turned to spring. On Valentine's day he had given her a present of 'Someday we'll be together' by the Supremes, which was out at the time. After the party, Joseph bitterly avoided Maura.

He continued to be one of the circle, playing in a garage band – with people who actually had a garage. They went on swimming trips to the open seawater pool at Seapoint, walking part of the way, small people made of nothing but energy, in the wide hot streets of the Southside. They dallied in a corner shop and picked up Calumet cigarettes to smoke on the way. There were camping expeditions with Matthew the cat-strangler, and Jack McCarthy, inventor of the clatter wank. Joseph used to ask for leniency as Jack tortured a younger Protestant kid they knew, who supported Chelsea, and cried easily.

They were on the Green. A couple of the girls had boys lying with their heads in the girls' laps. Joseph sat on one side, and Maura was standing nearby with her sister. The girls were playing 'I'm gonna make you mine' repeatedly on a red portable Dansette, and giggling at the 'Uh' sound in the middle.

Ida was a thin girl about their age, who was on student exchange from New York. She had bleach blonde hair and sat cross-legged revealing white knickers. She plucked a buttercup from the grass and showed them how to tell how highly-sexed somebody was by reflecting it on their elbows. As she was doing him, Joseph said 'Sex me!'

'In your dreams!' she said.

When he looked around, Maura had gone.

Ida was into Ten Year's After and The Beatles. Joseph was able to let her hear the new Let It Be album and she liked The Long and Winding Road best. He was not looking for a replacement for Maura, rather his attitude was 'Never again.' Ida found Joseph non-threatening enough to let him show her around town. They went to see the Book of Kells, and her reaction was 'Is that it?' In the glorious Botanical Gardens with its hothouses and hills, spanning the river Tolka, Ida said that the grounds of her school in New England were more impressive. The last thing that Joseph did for Ida, when she wanted to know where she could get acid, was to arrange for her to meet a dealer outside a jewellery shop in O'Connell Street.

Introducing the Old Member

Dave O'Reilly, moved into a house on the Green with his widowed mother, who doted on him. Dave was seventeen and the first of the blokes to have a car. His mother kept a shop, and they were comfortably off. Dave left school at an early age and worked on building sites. He liked to tell stories, in his Cavan accent, such as the revenge of the sacked bricklayers who broke into a site hut and shat in the teapot.

Dave was stocky, with a broad smile and nervously shaky hands. He was always in his garage or driveway working on the car, an open-topped Triumph Spitfire. He sprayed it yellow with a temperamental compressor, that had to be slapped on and off. Joseph hung out at Dave's place after the others had gone back to school. Lace curtains around the Green twitched, and snobbish parents must have warned their daughters off them.

A certain amount of drink had to be taken before dances in the local church halls. They were underage, of course, but were served without question upstairs in The Slipper as long as they kept quiet. The High Chaparral always seemed to be on, glaring blue on the screen above the bar. Joseph scandalised the exchange student girls at their table by telling them in French to sit on his face.

'*Qu'est-ce qu'il a dit?*'

The rock bands were so noisy in the church hall that all they could hear was a rumbling in their ears, no music. They emerged deaf into the night, to be greeted outside the gates by frightening skinheads in Crombey overcoats with roses in their buttonholes and Doc Marten boots, looking for 'odds.' The night could dissolve into a battle of flying chairs and bottles, when somebody looked askance at another drunk's girl. Another time a gang armed with weapons might race past chasing others down the empty, night-lit roads.

Sometimes they got to walk girls home. It turned out there were plenty of them willing to touch tongues, let Joseph put his hand inside their underwear, and very keen to do the same to him. One night sitting in Baretti's fish and chip café, with some of Dave's friends, Joseph watched one of the girls squeezing

Dave's leg under the table. Somebody allocated a girl called Nancy to Joseph, with much laughing. 'I'll walk you home,' he told her.

Not far into their walk they stopped to kiss. Joseph was a little bit sickened by the flavour of her chewing gum. If she was sickened by the taste of cigarettes on Joseph, it didn't stop her. Nancy had a great urge to stick her tongue rigidly down his throat. When they reached a secluded alleyway, they stopped and kissed again, with Joseph leaning his back on the wall. Nancy let him slip his fingers under her pubis into her wet hole, and she tugged on his hard penis. Somebody appeared in one end of the alley and they split up, never to meet again.

Nobody else in the neighbourhood at their age had a car. It was a bright evening when Dave and Joseph slowed down and asked some passing girls through the window if they wanted to go for a drink. Two of them got in and they drove out to Balbriggan on the coast, and got the girls drunk. They were in a club bar with the kind of lighting that makes underwear shine through clothes. Dave's one was so drunk she tried to get out of the passenger door at about forty miles per hour on the Swords road.

Joseph struck lucky with Hazel in the back seat, when they parked up. She had next to nothing in her bra, so she guided his hand straight down to her watering vulva, as they twined and slithered their tongues together. 'I don't always do this, I'm usually very strict,' she said as he explored her, and she stroked his erection. Dave turned to look in at the two in the backseat. 'Are you introducing her to your old member?' He was not getting as far with his bird. They never met her or Hazel again.

It was known about every girl in the neighbourhood, and for miles around, 'how far she would go'. Dave graduated to bedding girls with derogatory nicknames like Fishface, in the house that he had to himself by day while his mother worked in the shop. Joseph gravitated towards the nicer type of girls, and so remained a virgin, getting at most a chaste kiss goodnight.

Mrs O'Reilly gave Dave a brand-new car for his eighteenth birthday. Joseph and Dave went in it for an overnight trip to Dave's old family farm, near the border in Cavan. The local dancehall was big and there was a showband playing a bit of rock and roll, a bit of Tom Jones, and a bit of Country and Irish. It was more of a spectacle than a chance to pull. There were distances between groups in the hall.

On their way back into the night countryside they sped past a black car full of local lads. It was waiting to come out of a sideroad. The locals followed and started racing them. Dave floored the accelerator, and they were soon belting down the pitch-black country roads with the speedometer touching eighty miles per hour. They hit a straight where the road was being resurfaced. The other car got in front of them, and stones started hitting the windscreen. Joseph crouched down in the passenger seat.

It wasn't much of a surprise to hear one day that Dave O'Reilly had written off his new car in a head-on crash with a coach on a narrow bend. He was in hospital for a long time, and during his stay Mrs O'Reilly moved them out of the house on the Green.

Coda

Maura ended up marrying Jack McCarthy, who became a merchant seaman. Many years later on a visit home to Dublin, Joseph thought he caught a glimpse of her as he was driving by on the other side. It was outside the house where Jack's family used to live. She appeared to be waiting for somebody and looking at the ground. Joseph wondered if she ever heard 'Someday we'll be together' on the radio or if she still kept the record and when she played it, did she think of him.

Emmet Swan

Brother Sebastian looked askance at the boy and said in a nasal voice, 'He shows a slight tendency towards effeminacy.' Brother Sebastian always looked askance at boys with long hair. Emmet's was shoulder-length and black, and he had an atom of the orient in his eyes.

As headmaster of the secondary school, Brother Sebastian felt it was his place to make them squirm for a while before approving their application. He grunted over details about how Emmet had ended up living with his uncle, while Emmet's mother was away in another country. Emmet wore a perplexed expression throughout the ordeal. Brother Sebastian showed them out, leaning strangely to one side as if about to reach for a gun in his clerical cassock.

Emmet's uncle said it was only a formality. When they got home, Emmet went to the Shopping Parade where a few older boys were talking about stealing a car. One of them called Hawkeye was showing off a bunch of a hundred odd car keys. Emmet soon found himself in the back of a stolen Ford Cortina, barrelling over the blackened wooden causeway onto Dollymount Strand. The driver raced the car towards the sea, which was miles out, then spun it around and back in toward the dunes. The car bogged down in soft sand, so they abandoned it and walked along a track through the marram grass. In the middle of the dunes they lay down, and somebody passed a joint around.

After dragging on the joint, his first, a feeling of endlessly receding from the group came over Emmet. He was not listening to what they were saying, just looking at their mouths moving. He left them and walked to the main road where he started hitch-hiking. A fat man on a Honda 90 motorbike already sagging under the weight pulled over. Emmet hardly fit on the back, and as the bike got up to speed, he turned his face up to the sun with his straight hair streaming in the wind and laughed out loud.

From the start of first year, Emmet got more from and brought more to the lessons, than the other students at St. Floncus secondary school. He grew bored with the lessons and turned his attention to studies of his own devising. When they learned about explosives in Chemistry, Emmet did some extra-curricular homework in his uncle's workshop with Hawkeye. They put a piece of copper pipe in the bench vice, and filled it with a mixture of garden and kitchen ingredients. Not long afterwards, a loud bang from the garden. Scared old people peeked through lace curtains in the neighbouring terraces of ex-army cottages. Hawkeye had gone home earlier. Emmet, already a block away, decided to go for a long walk.

By second year, he would hold court on the step outside the school canteen, where his followers collected to hear jokes, tales of joyriding, plots to slip LSD into the Brothers' milk supply and anything he cared to relate. Just being tall and confident would have been enough to bring him followers. But it was his conversation that held and amazed them. He seemed to be several years more mature, easily making the excitable second years laugh and chatter.

On this day, he gathered a group around him and told the story of the spider that eventually went deaf when its legs were pulled off one by one. Nobody thought of the cruelty, or that it must have been somebody else's joke. All they knew was that here was somebody very clever. They tried to share in the cleverness by repeating 'Spider, walk!' for days.

Joseph Murphy didn't say much because he was only a newcomer who had joined late in first year – not that he would have anyway.

There was chaos in the prefab classroom that Joseph landed in. Brother Sebastian, the Head, came in to lecture them about graffiti that had appeared on a wall near the main entrance, 'Mr. Gillow is a queer.' Mr. Gillow was a Civics teacher, with an eye-squinting smile. As Brother Sebastian lectured, he walked up and down the rows of desks waving a heavy steel ruler absent-mindedly. As he turned the corner of the back row, he suddenly slapped the ruler hard on Emmet's desk, flat side down making a loud bang. Brother Sebastian, nicknamed Slimy, swayed and looked at the ruler in his hand as if shocked that it had appeared there. Emmet blanked him with a sardonic smile.

As soon as Slimy left the room, spitballs of chewed-up paper were fired from sprung steel rulers by the sport-loving knuckleheads at the front of the room, over the silent majority towards the back, where Joseph skulked along with Emmet and other long-haired malingerers. Emmet was big enough to take on the knuckleheads, and went on the attack, clambering over desktops into the front line.

'I thought they didn't allow those,' Joseph said, about the name bracelet that Emmet was wearing. 'I had one at my interview, and Slimy said it showed a tendency to effeminacy.'

'Bollox!' said Emmet. 'He said the same thing to me.'

After that Joseph put his name bracelet back on, and resumed wearing what he thought of as his Sgt. Peppers uniform jacket – though it was far from that – a double-breasted thing with silver buttons.

The Religion teacher, Brother Louis, organised an election for class Captain and Vice-Captain. Votes were to be written anonymously on slips of paper which were then counted by two volunteers. As Joseph hardly knew the names of any other boys, he voted for

'Anarchy.' Brother Louis was about sixty inches tall, with a gnarled face. He had been pressganged into the Brothers at the age of sixteen, resulting in a sour and bloody-minded disposition.

'Who is responsible for writing "Anarchy"?' he demanded.

Joseph put his hand up, like George Washington.

'All it takes is one bad apple, to spoil the whole barrel,' Brother Louis said.

He never looked at Joseph or spoke to him again, and only referred to him indirectly as a target for snide remarks, for the rest of the year. Joseph thought about asking to be excused from Religion, but instead he went through the motions every day, standing up, pretending to pray at the beginning and end of Louis' class.

Brother 'Baldy' Eustace was a plodding teacher, not wholly ineffectual but handicapped by a plummy voice with exceptionally contorted diphthongs and, as his nickname implied, a glaring bonce. For no reason Baldy got it into his head that Joseph Murphy was behind some disruption. As Joseph was leaving his class one morning, Baldy grabbed him by the hair and pushed him heavily against the wall of the corridor.

'You young blatherskite,' he snarled, 'You will come to a bad end!'

They were so bored. Emmet would start crossing out words and letters in textbooks to make humorous variants, handing them across the rows to Joseph, who would elaborate the travesties and pass them back. At each stop in the human chain, laughter would burst out when they read the words. Emmet started a series of cartoons featuring a transgenic creature, a palm tree with floppy leaves on top and kangaroo feet, and called it a Kangabanana.

Brother Jack – as diminutive as Louis but sweeter – took the religion class occasionally, and there were interesting discussions on his shift. One day Emmet asked Brother Jack if it was okay for homosexuals to marry. Brother Jack wiggled his hand, and waffled about how although it was a difficult subject, if they kept to the rules and brought up their children in the church and so on, it would probably be okay.

'No,' said Emmet, 'I mean is it allowed for them to marry each other?'

When they came back for third year, there were illicit expeditions by the longhaired malingerers to the nearby shops, and lunchtimes spent in the out-of-bounds pool hall. When the pool hall manager was leaned on to stop letting them in, they took to sitting in the tiled doorway of the nearby pub or anywhere along the parade of small shops. People called them 'the hooligans.' They followed Emmet out down the lane, exactly like disciples. Joseph sometimes dreamed of taking Emmet's place and making him his John the Baptist.

Some of the other boys had access to money and drugs. Dwyer who only had one good eye, was bullied unmercifully, and tried to gain kudos by taking more and better drugs than the rest. They called him Cyclops. Emmet was not above twisting Dwyer's arm behind his back to extort money or cigarettes, though there was pained laughter on both sides. The local shopkeepers watched them carefully, rightly suspecting some of them of slipping items under coats, as they browsed and eventually got a Granny's Ginger Cake or Australian Sultana Cake to eat in the street.

Appointments would be made to meet up with contacts outside the gates of Trinity College, say, who would supply them with dope. Cyclops, formerly a star pupil always volunteering answers, started missing a lot of days. Eventually he had difficulty answering any questions at all. They said he was on LSD. Cyclops's parents kicked him out of their house and he stopped coming to school.

During the summer holiday, Joseph had become a singer in a garage band, The Bloody Fools, and played guitar two strings at a time up and down the frets. He handed Emmet a tape of songs recorded by the band on a C30 cassette. Emmet said he liked the titles written on the cassette case, though it was nearly impossible to make out anything from the sound on the cassette. Joseph was talking and stumbling, trying to keep up with him. He had heard something about Emmet's Bible, a collection of poems, and wondered if he could set one to music. Emmet gave him a handwritten poem about a Christmas funeral, to turn into a song.

Joseph was clumsy, which Emmet found amusing,

but Joseph was not the type of kid who could be bullied. When they were smuggling stuff down the corridor and Coke sloshed from a bottle in Joseph's inside pocket onto the parquet floor Emmet quipped, 'Why did I have to pick somebody with spring in his step?' On their way to Joseph's place to let Emmet hear the song, after they crossed Floncus Avenue, Joseph tripped over the kerb and Emmet laughed.

It was late that autumn, when The Bloody Fools performed, sans drummer, at the Coffee Kitchen folk club in Molesworth Street. It was in a dim basement room, overcrowded and dripping condensation from the painted ceiling and walls. The turns drank in a nearby pub or waited outside in half-dark below the street railings. On one side a duo called McWreck were testing unusual open tunings on their guitars. Stack, the genius of the northside was comparing blues riffs with a visiting American Joan Baez type. It was enough to make The Bloody Fools ordinary tuning-up seem shamefully humble. Emmet showed up with Cyclops, probably expecting to hear his song. Joseph went out into the Street and sat on the steps with them. They laughed at Cyclops for getting high on a fake herbal mixture someone gave them; he was sure it was good stuff, as he sucked in through his teeth.

When third year was ending, Careers Advisors were all over them. Like Cyclops, Emmet had started to miss days. In Emmet's interview, the Careers teacher told him he was probably insane and needed help. Emmet was hurt and developed the heavy demeanour of a worried man.

In the sixth-year smoking room, though it was supposed to be out-of-bounds for third-years, they discussed topics such as how to pilfer lab equipment to use for microphone stands. In one corner, somebody was brandishing a real Wyatt Earp length handgun. A panel of the outer door was booted in, and some joker held up a porn magazine centrefold in the gap. Emmet and Joseph balanced their long cigarette ash, and returned to their conversation.

Emmet was in love with a girl called Joan. Her father hated Emmet for his long hair.

'He calls me the neighbourhood Danny La Rue,' Emmet said to Joseph, 'but don't tell anybody I told you that.'

Soon Joan was pregnant. There was no going back to school for Emmet now and all kinds of drugs were going down; not just cannabis, but mescaline, mandrax and acid too. It was a springtime of Afghan coats, buying and smoking dope in places like the Common Room above the gatehouse of Trinity College, where weak shafts of sunlight fanned over old, dark furniture; or down basements of joss sticks, ready beds and strapping country girls. Sick kids slumped in street doorways, zonked on cheap, potent cough medicine.

Joseph went to Emmet's house to collect another poem to set to music. They left Emmet's uncle dozing with slippers and newspaper in a back room and walked up the road to get Joan. Emmet toyed with the harmonium in her parlour while they waited for her. The three of them returned to Emmet's front room and put on some Pentangle music, and later Simon & Garfunkel and Jefferson Airplane.

They were smoking pale Lebanese dope neat in an improvised pipe. Emmet passed it to Joan, who passed it back. Emmet reached the pipe over to Joseph who took his first ever toke and immediately hallucinated. Emmet and Joan's faces seemed to spin rapidly like slot machine dials with alternating images of Olive Oyle and Popeye on them.

Another guy came in, wired-up on speed and started rabbiting. Joseph was trying to tell them how he felt like a painting hanging on a wall with nothing at all behind him, no back to his head. He felt as if his voice was being smothered under a pile of pillows. The wired-up guy started grouching about Joseph playing 'head games.'

Somebody put on a Beach Boys single that Joseph said was really cool. He walked the four miles home mostly thinking about what he was feeling like. So this was it, he was a true disciple at last. He found the Beach Boys single in the pocket of his army surplus jacket when he reached home, together with a handwritten poem, 'A prayer for Joan and the winter conceived.'

None of them went back to St Floncus for fourth year. The last time he saw Emmet was on the south side of town. He was wearing a dark sleeveless Afghan, and looking weary and wounded. They stopped by a second-floor bedsit where Emmet was semi-domesticated with Joan. They had to get out of there and walk. Emmet was talking about starting an 'underground' magazine. Why underground, Joseph wondered – but didn't say.

When they got to the north end of town, they stopped and sat on a bench in the Garden of Remembrance. A multi-coated tramp came in, took off one boot and submerged it in the raised pond right in front of them, poured out the water, put it back on and then started on the other boot. For a moment the cloud lifted from Emmet's face and there was that sardonic smile again. He said, 'These strange things only happen when you're around, Joe!'

That was the last time he ever saw Emmet Swan. He ran into Cyclops a couple of years later, and learned that Emmet was in a Spanish jail for smuggling dope from Morocco. Cooking gas canisters are supposed to be cold to the touch, apparently.

Truant

'I take it that most of you will be transferring to our own secondary school,' said Brother John. 'Is there anyone who isn't?'

Joseph Murphy put his hand up.

'Joseph, are you leaving us?'

'I might be going to St. Myles.'

'Oh, that's quite a famous one. It's all-Irish; do you think you'll be able to manage?'

'I've got the scholarship, to pay for it.'

'Well you are a star in the Irish anyway. And what advantages would you say it has over our own St. Floncus?'

Joseph remembered what his father had read in the newspaper.

'They've just built a new wing for science.'

'Is that so? Well then you're going to be a scientist instead of a writer, after building up our hopes with your compositions!'

. . .

It was a Monday in late September. The green double-decker trundled townward between bus-high trees. The yellowing leaves whirled and lingered in Joseph's mind with all the street images, like rosary beads to a believer.

Ahead of him the pupils would already be filing into the creaking ark of St. Myles to study moribund Gaelic dialects, while outside it rained English. The place would reek as usual of burnt soup, as they swarmed up wide oak stairs.

He would have to spend his day queuing, either for food or for punishment, to get up the stairs or to bound over a wooden horse. He wouldn't queue at the urinals though, outside in the yard where one wall was lined with them. He would have to hold it in all day, because he couldn't relax enough to perform in public, and even the nearby stalls with their half doors did not feel private.

He had Latin taught through Irish to look forward to, to dread – one dead language via another comatose one. Brother Feargal was there waiting for them to sit down in the filthy old flip-top desks. His puce-coloured hatchet face was connected by flapping tendons in his neck to the split white bib of the Christian Brothers black cassock. As they struggled to their places, all trying to avoid one unfortunate kid who stank of piss, Feargal would be warning them about the conjugations they were supposed to have memorised.

One by one Feargal would lead them to a question they couldn't answer, and they would have to stand at the wall, till the whole class was standing. He would teach them a lesson. The worst offenders would be segregated on one side from the rest. Feargal would pass along the line of the worst dunces administering a hefty whack with his leather strap to the boys' outheld palms. Joseph had been lucky so far, only to stand in the average dunces line. He couldn't face the strap, which was like a barber's sharpening strop, a thick strip of leather with a curved hilt.

English at least was not through Irish, but at the end of the first week there had been no essay, and there was no prospect of one. Joseph had no chance to show his ability, he was assumed to be as insignificant as the rest, a child. It is hard when you feel grown up to be treated like a child. Quinn, the teacher was a small, scruffy layman, who crouched on top of Joseph's desk. His lessons offered no promise of anything other than pedantry and boredom.

Joseph saw his stop late, as the crowded bus passed by Parnell Square. He stayed seated. By the next stop he knew he would be late if he went back, and he couldn't face the Christian Brothers' pitiless straps. He had only been singled out for the strap once in all his years with the De La Salle brothers in Primary and that had been devastating. So he stayed where he was, while the bus continued through the city centre, and he got off after it reached Trinity College across the river.

He put his schoolbag out of sight at the back of a deep hedgerow in St Stephen's Green so no school inspectors or policeman would think he was supposed to be in school. There was never a question of going back to St. Myles the next day – worse punishment would only follow. So every day Joseph walked the streets, and kept an eye on public clocks to bus-it home in time for lunch, and in the evening as if after school.

Joseph reached Grafton Street on the morning after Piggotts music shop burned down. There were skips full of charred wood, strings and broken junk outside. He stood in the cordoned-off street looking up at the blackened shell of the building. An office worker passing by fished a tin whistle from one of the skips, and looked at it before dropping it in a litter bin. Joseph picked it up and put it in his pocket.

'From Pigotts!' his mother said, when he showed her. She had heard about the fire on the news. 'How did you get that? What were you doing there?'

'No, I wasn't there. One of the fellas in our class passes by there. He had three of them with him this morning and he gave me one.'

By night he stayed in his room alone, pretending to do homework – the only time his schoolbag was ever opened. It was for that extra bedroom that his family had moved to the new estate, but Joseph had no friends on the new estate and at the same time he had transferred to a school where he didn't know anybody either.

The days were getting shorter. Footpaths frosted over. The nearest he came to studying was by using

Eason's bookstore. He was standing reading John Lennon In His Own Write, and just about to finish it when an assistant said 'This is not a library.' He was afraid to use Kevin Street library in case they reported him for being off school every day.

Joseph was leaning on a tree, beside the lake in St. Stephen's Green. It had been raining earlier in the morning and the ground was still damp. A small, not quite elderly man in an overcoat appeared, feeding birds with bits of bread from a paper bag. He looked Joseph up and down.

'Nice day, cleared up grand,' the man began.

'Mmm,' was all that Joseph said.

Joseph was wearing a sleeveless fairisle top over his school shirt, standard issue dark navy blazer and school-grey slacks. His hair was still wet and plastered down from the rain, in a broken fringe.

'The gulls are a terror,' said the man, 'I favour the ducks but it's no use. Is this your first time in here?'

'No.'

'I suppose you have the day off school?'

'Mmm.'

'Why's that?' the man kept on, 'Teachers' meeting or something, I suppose. They seem to have a great time of it these days, the teachers. I'm sure I've seen you here a few times. You must have a lot of days off. You know what I think – it's not a day off at all, eh? And they let you wander here on your own. Do you live near here?'

He told the man where they lived, and about the new house.

'That's a long way! What's your name?'

'Joseph.'

'Which way are you going now, Joe?'

'I have to go home for my lunch in a few minutes.'

'I'm just going over here,' the almost elderly man nodded, 'Are you coming?'

They went over the shady stone bridge down between the flower beds and the hissing fountains.

'Have you got any sisters, Joe?' This man had a lot of questions.

'Yes.'

'Younger or older?'

Joseph did not feel like answering any more questions. They sat down on a park bench on the far side of the park.

'Have you got any dirty books at home,' the man came out with, and leaned towards Joseph.

'Well 'The Carpetbaggers' used to be lying around, and I read most of that,' said Joseph.

'I'm surprised they let you read that.'

'They hid it away, but I found it again.'

'And did that make you horny?' said the overcoated, not quite elderly man. 'Did that make the little man stand up?'

'Yes.'

'And did you like that?' said the man.

170

'Yes.'

'You ought to see the filthy dirty books that I have in my room. He'll really go mad.'

'I have to go now,' said Joseph, and started to leave.

'I could sell you one if you come back after dinner.'

'Okay.'

'I'll bring it with me then. Meet me here at two o'clock. Don't forget, will you.'

It was raining again that afternoon. Joseph sat in the cavern-like shelter facing the fountains in the middle of the park. A shadow from far along the semi-circular bench shuffled nearer. Joseph saw the lunatic eyes and shock of red hair of a stocky young man. He gave Joseph a cigarette, and then started straight into his questions.

'Did you meet any queers? There are a lot of queers around this place.'

Joseph was surprised to hear the Enid Blyton word 'queer' used in this way.

'I met an oulfella this morning,' Joseph said, guessing, 'I was supposed to meet him here at two o'clock. I didn't want to. But anyway he wasn't there.'

'It must have been D. What was he like?'

'A little oulfella in a grey coat.'

'Yeah, that's him. I know him. Did he ask you up to his room?'

'Yes. But I didn't want to,' said Joseph.

'Good. Never go with them,' said the red-haired man.

'He said he'd sell me a dirty book.'

'But you have no money,' said the red-haired man. 'Some of them hang around the public toilets. Whatever you do, don't let them get you in there. They could be very nice and bring you in and then kick the bollix out of you. It has happened.'

The red-haired man smirked all the time and spoke animatedly.

'Stick with me, I'll see you're all right,' he said.

When it stopped raining, Joseph headed back out through the main gate at the northwest corner of the park, with the red-haired man tagging alongside. He kept in with Joseph by giving him another cigarette. If it were not for that, Joseph could have ditched him. Once he'd got the cigarette lit, Joseph turned south along the pavement beside the black railings, that held in the trees and deep shrubbery of the park. If he had turned east, they would have had to pass by where the schoolbag was hidden.

'How would you like to be an actor?' the red-haired man went on, dogging him. 'Actors are all queers you know. I did a bit of acting myself, joined Equity, went to Ardmore for a day and saw them all.'

'What do you work at now?' Joseph asked.

'Do you think I'm a dosser!' the man was angry now. 'Do you think I'm a queer? Do I look like a queer!'

'Sorry, I don't know. It's no use asking me.'

Joseph turned around and walked back north along Grafton Street.

'I could drag you down there somewhere now and no one would bother to help you,' the man said as they passed by an alleyway.

The red-haired man edged to turn right down the next side street, gesturing for Joseph to follow.

'There's a place I know down this way where we could have a cup of coffee. Are you coming?'

'No I have to watch the clock,' Joseph said, deciding to stay on the main street, and walked away.

Joseph hoped he wouldn't see the red-haired man again. Come Thursday of the following week, just when he thought he was in the clear, he ran into him in Grafton Street again on his way to the park. The man took up where he left off.

'Are you going to the park?'

'No,' Joseph said, and doubled back northwards.

'Do you know what a wank is?' the red-haired man asked, walking alongside.

'No.'

'Do you never pull at yourself till the jip comes out?'

'Yes.'

'Well that's a wank you're having. "Masturbation" it's called. Where does the jip go?'

'In the sheets.' Joseph couldn't see why the man was so interested. It wasn't anything special.

'Oh no, you shouldn't do that. Your mother will find out. You mark my words, she will find out what you're doing. What size is it?' The red-haired man made a size with his hand. 'About that? Or that?' Joseph looked around.

'Yes.'

'How long does it take to come off?'

'Em, about three minutes.' It made no sense. There was nothing for the man to smile about.

'It's much better if you do it with your left hand, it feels like somebody else is doing it. Did you ever do it with an apple?'

'No.'

'Do you not know that? You get an apple, make a hole in it and put plenty of you know that Pond's cold cream. It's fucken brilliant.'

They had just passed by the Grafton cartoon cinema.

'Do you like Cartoons? We could go in there and watch whatever's on,' the man said. 'I saw an oulfella in there one time with his hand in this other lad's trousers. I think I'll go in, are you coming?'

'No.'

'Come on!'

Joseph visualized the cartoon cinema virtually empty for the Thursday matinee. He veered off Grafton Street into Woolworths, one of his usual beats.

'Can I have a cigarette,' Joseph asked.

'Here!' said the red-haired man, following.

They were inside Woolworths now. Joseph stopped to get a light from him, and then stepped onto the escalator.

'Are you not coming?' the red-haired man demanded, rooted at the bottom of the escalator.

Joseph shook his head, carried on smoking and the red-haired man receded out of view. On the upper floor of Woolworths, Joseph surveyed the mirrored stalls where the snack biscuits were, and wondered if he could get away with stealing one. After touring the hardware department, he went back down via the staircase on the other side. There was no sign of the red-haired man.

It was a December evening and Joseph went to collect his schoolbag. It had been raided. Scrabbling through undergrowth in the hiding place, he found the empty bag and a scattering of torn pages. On one of the pages there was a scribbled message, 'Ha ha we hide our bags too but we pick a better place.' Running before the park would close, Joseph caught up with a park warden and asked him if he had found any books. The warden said no, and the park was closing. Joseph followed the warden on his rounds for a while, but the warden told him to go out of the park.

5:30 p.m. and it was dark already. Joseph waited with his father at the hall door outside St Myles secondary school. Beside them a high-windowed room spilled light out over black railings. They were shown into the office. The Principal rose from his big desk to greet them, and closed the curtains.

'What is it, in three years they do the Inter. Cert, isn't it?' said Joseph's father as an ice-breaker.

'Yes,' said the Principal. 'And then either two or three

years to the Leaving Cert. What age is Joseph now?'

'He's thirteen.'

'I see. We prefer to let them take the Leaving Cert at eighteen. We find that the extra year is a great help to them. They are more mature. Let's see.' He muttered a calculation. 'So in sixth year he would be eighteen. Some schools skip the fourth year, but that would mean doing the Leaving Cert. at seventeen. However, I needn't tell you that everything depends on Joseph's attendance. From now on it will have to be impeccable.'

'I think he's fairly determined now,' Joseph's father said, with a little nod.

'Good,' said the Principal. 'Well that is the only way we could see to accept him back, you understand. It's a terrible thing to see young boys wandering around the streets alone. You know this city is not what it was like when you and I were young.' He paused and lowered his voice. 'There are a lot of homosexuals about.'

'Oh, I'd say that, right enough.'

'I don't have to tell you that just one encounter could ruin a boy for life.'

The Silver Circle

The Brothers held a weekly raffle called the Silver Circle, with the primary school children as their runners. Joseph Murphy counted the addresses on his card again – less than a page full, and some of those hardly ever paid. It was amazing that other boys had forty-five good ones. They would be allowed to keep sixpence for every page of twenty. He looked at his lines: Glencree Road, MacDonagh Road, Casement Avenue. No purchase houses, that was the problem. There was only one car in his street, a black Ford Popular with running boards. He closed the textured blue card, with its holy logo. 'I'm just going to collect my Silver Circle,' he called out, but they were having their Saturday morning lie-in.

Joseph in the rain, barely light morning, the concrete a palette of greys. Rapids in the gutter. Knock and give the code words 'Is your mammy in?' to the kids who answered. Sometimes it was hard to tell. Discussion could be heard with coarse male voices. Many times no answer came, although clearly there was someone home. Others frankly admitted they could not afford the sixpence this week. Little zeros instead of ticks in the column. 'Another duck!' Brother Nicholas would exclaim, as he checked against the number of coins handed in when the children lined up with their returns.

The parish of St. Floncus was a frontier territory where disused farms met pebbledashed houses. Green algae clogged ditches of frog spawn and tadpoles. Stopcock shores made dungeons for bees the kids captured in jam jars. Rivers that rose in the gutters in torrential rain, when the drops splashed off the ground, were waterways for sailing ice-pop sticks.

Joseph walked through a gap in the bramble hedgerow to cross to the lower reaches of Corporation terraces in South Finglas. Ahead lay the fields, thistled and wet, with vinegar plants and dock leaves in the grass. Tinkers' horses ruminated, tethered or sometimes free. It was a local sport for rough boys to rope them and ride bareback. In the back of his mind were stories about gangs from West Finglas who would torture you with burning sticks. The kind of boys who got a kick out of throwing a cat on a fire.

On every edge of the suburbs were hayfields, waste lands, ditches and culverts. There was a sense of adventure and foreboding, never knowing what would lie on the other side of a hill. The animals were mostly tame, but some of the people were wild. Children were left to wander in a wilderness of cliffs and river gorges, when they were supposed to be in school. The travelling people came and went leaving a trail of unwanted clothes.

What you would call a bluff maybe, he had just crested, and there to one side stood a wire-haired young man, lashing a tethered horse with a rope, so that the horse ran as it could, only in a circle around its stake. Joseph knew instantly that there was no way in the world he was going to get past without paying some sort of toll.

'What are you looking at?' the man snapped. It was the standard impossible question. It was certain he would take exception to whatever answer Joseph gave.

'I said what are you looking at!'

No answer at all would be worse.

'Nothing.'

'Are you calling me nothing? Come here!'

Seeing it would be futile to run and the horse man was already walking towards him, Joseph paused. Before he had time to think, the man had come and hit him in the face. Joseph dropped to one knee, blood trickling from his nose. He wiped the blood away with the back of his hand. The man stood over him, holding a doubled rope poised like a whip.

'What's that?' he demanded, pointing at the blue card in Joseph's hand.

'It's just the Silver Circle,' said Joseph, 'I'm collecting for it.'

The man raised the rope to strike but refrained,

smirking, half surprised and half amused to find in himself a twinge of pity.

'I could kill you here and nobody would know,' he said. 'Hand over the money!'

'I can't,' Joseph said. 'It's for the Silver Circle.'

But even as he was saying it, Joseph was turning out his pockets. He handed the coins to the man who then walked away and resumed baiting the small black and white horse. Joseph pushed on through hoofprints and knotted grass, till he was out of sight, and then ran.

The way to the Brothers' house was through the school playing fields, along a path lined with poplars. He was late and the prefab classroom where they queued to hand in the money was closed, so he had to go to the house. It was secluded from the school by evergreens on three sides, and from the street beyond by a ten-foot wall. Entering the gardens Joseph passed by a large aviary, neat vegetable plots and flower beds. Ahead, at the end of the path, steps led up to double doors standing open. In a large office near the entrance, Brother Nicholas sat behind a leather-topped desk. Seeing Joseph knock at the open door, he closed a drawer under the desk. There was a clinking sound of bottle and glass sliding together.

'Enter!'

He continued writing something in a ledger, balancing columns of pounds, shillings and pence.

'Well,' Brother Nicholas said eventually, looking up with an exaggerated grin. 'And what have you got for us this week Mr. Murphy?'

'The money was st-st-stolen, Brother.'

'The money was st-st-stolen,' Nicholas mimicked in a little voice. 'Well somebody will have to pay. And how did this happen, pray tell?'

'A fellow beat me up and t-t-took the money, when I was crossing the fields, Brother.'

'Did he indeed?' he said. 'A likely story!'

I Must Be an Indian

Wanted Criminals

Joseph says, I hate the noise of drills in the morning. How are we supposed to sleep? And they put me in a separate bed that folds up. It's called a tallboy. I am as big as a house now. I always wet the bed. It's a big problem.

I know when people are falling asleep. It's when their breath goes slower. First it goes faster and faster. In out in out in out. Then it changes and goes In...no out. In...no out. Slower and slower. Sometimes they make a gurgling sound and then they stop making sound. That's when they're asleep.

Granda says he's going to see a man about a dog. For me, yes for me. He puts flame in a pipe and drinks it. Pop...Pop. A big cloud comes out and makes my throat sore. Bulldog is the kind I want, and that's just what the man in the pub has, bulldogs. I know where the pub is. It's called the Long Hall. I can see the back of it from the landing window. I don't know which one it is though.

Granda has his bed on one side of the room and we all slept in a big bed on the other side before. The cooker is on the other side and the window is on the other side. I have told you all the sides now, four. I can count. Mammy and Daddy were at the top of the bed, and me and my sister at their feet. We had to keep moving to find a comfy place.

When it is too cold Granda puts his overcoat on top of the blankets. It smells like sacks of coal, because Granda used to bring home a few pieces of coal in his pocket that fell out of the sacks in his work. I like it, it's better than blankets. There is a sign on the shop outside our window. It says 'Keys.' I can spell. It's pink and it keeps going on and off. I am able to see it all night.

'Where does the music come from, Mammy?'

'From the ice rink, Joseph.'

I know what an ice rink is now. It's where the boys dance with the girls. I know how to sing all the songs. My favourite is 'Put your sweet lips' because it's lovely and loud and soft. But the ones with the most words are 'That yellow dress' and 'Things like a walk in the park' and I can sing them all. I never stop singing till I fall asleep.

I didn't mind when we moved to Granda's because I got a friend in the street called Martin. We play in the street, Martin and me.

'Do you know what women's big things in the front are called – diddies,' Martin said.

'Yeah, I know. Diddies.'

'Diddies, diddies, diddies,' we shouted and laughed.

Mammy heard us and opened the window.

'Stop that dirty talk the pair of yous! I heard yous.'

On the corner a fat woman sells fruit from a barrow. Her dress is big enough to hide things under. I saw rotten apples underneath the barrow. Martin said she pisses on them. He says when people pass by who don't know her, she gives them some good apples from the top and one pissy one from underneath. She shouts 'penny apples,' but Martin says they're not even worth a penny.

Dockrells' shop is where we're not allowed to go. It's across a big street. But we still go to look in the windows.

'I must get this and you must get that,' we say.

'I must get the Indian outfit and you must get the cowboy outfit,' Martin said.

'I must get the gun and you must get the bow and arrow,' I said.

At Christmas the children in the street had their outfits. I went down to play with them but I couldn't play properly because I only had a holster and no gun.

One time I stayed in Martin's house and I was afraid I would wet the bed, but I didn't. They have more than one room. At breakfast they fold their bread long ways, not like us. It's very clever that way. I will fold my bread that way now. Martin has beautiful sisters. I said they look like two Japanese dolls! His parents looked at me a lot when I said that.

I shouldn't have told you my friend's name. The police are after us. We have to be very careful and check up and down the street before going out. It's all because one day we were playing sliding down the windscreen of cars, in a stony place up the other end of the street. We were trying smoking cigarette butts too. I don't know if it was the smoking or the sliding on the windscreens, anyway a policeman came round the corner. We knew he was a superintendent by his grey uniform. One of the boys said, 'L.O.B.' and then 'Scatter.' The superintendent shouted and came after us. We ran away back down the street very fast. He is still looking for us.

In summer it gets so hot the tar melts in between the concrete on the road. It's great for making men out of. We sit on the kerb up near the stony car park, just near the corner and pull the tar out, then make it into things.

I saw other boys with bamboo canes. You can make fishing rods with them and nylons, to catch pinkeens in the park. They said they got them from Dockrells' warehouse, so I went to look. There was a tall box full of bamboo canes sticking up inside the open gates. I waited to see if somebody would give me some too, but nobody did so I ran home.

The Age of Reason

We practised getting communion. Miss showed us a

golden plate called a paten. That just proves how precious the Host is because the altar boys have to catch any crumbs.

'What happens to the crumbs?'

'The priest will take them later, Joseph. Now these are only wafers, they are so you can learn how to receive the sacrament.'

We have to stick our tongues out and say, 'Amen' when the priest says 'Corpus Christi.' It's hard to get the words out and stick your tongue out, without making a mistake and doing them together. We have to let the wafer dissolve. No chewing. It sticks to my mouth till it gets soggy. That's when I can swallow it.

There are mortal sins and venial sins. We are only seven, so Miss says we only have venial sins because none of us has committed murder yet, or coveted our neighbours' wives. We have to count all the lies we told and the times we answered our mammies back. Even curses, but they are very bad, so go easy with them. Think carefully, count the number. There is a lot of thinking. Before you go in, to remember your sins. Then when you come out you have to bow your head and say your penance. Miss says if we're not really sorry, we won't really be forgiven, and we will go to Hell.

You have to remember all the words to say. 'Bless me Father, for I have sinned. This is my First Confession. I told lies four times, and I answered me ma back once in the last week.' It's hard to think of enough sins. You have to have about four, at least, and different kinds. If you get fed up trying to think of them, you can just make them up. Nobody will ever know.

In first class we have Miss for our teacher. If she's not in we go into second class and the nun stands at the front and says prayers. One time I kneeled beside her and used the black rosary beads hanging from her waist for praying.

'Look what a good boy this is everybody,' said Sister. 'What's your name?'

I don't even know who everybody is. I only can see Sister's black dress. She has a big cross on her front, and a big black and white thing on her head.

I got new Little Duke shoes, and a suit with a medal ribbon on it. I am about half as tall as the mangle in the yard where the toilets are. That's where all the gulls come down laughing and crying when it's going to rain. But it is sunny today. The sky is high up not low down. When we are big we will be able to wear longers, but not yet. I can't swing on the rope or anything like that today in the yard because of my clean clothes.

It's quite funny going around all the doors with Mammy and they all say how lovely I look, a handsome devil, and give me money. Some of them give me orange paper money. Mammy minds that for me. But I can keep the silver. Well, I don't need all of it, just enough for a child. I am rich.

The priests made a big dinner in the school, and all the communion girls and boys sat at long tables. There was jelly and custard. They were very happy with us. But I don't know anybody here, only me. After that, they let us go. Our school is called Clarendon Street, and the way I go home is called Messer Street.

There was no traffic, no bicycles and the street is only small but the buildings are big. There were a lot of toys in a shop window. I asked the man in the shop what I could get for my money, and I showed him how much. He showed me some things, so I decided to get a fishing rod set. He said okay, and before you go you can afford one of these too, and he gave me a parachute man.

So I carried the fishing rod set, and opened the parachute man package outside the shop. Then I pointed it up at the blue sky and blew it. The parachute man flew into the air and floated down into the middle of the road. So I put him back in the tube and blew it again, and he floated far. Every time I pointed him up at the blue sky and he parachuted down far, all the way home.

The Beginning

Joseph says, I never saw such a low window before. It's like being in the street. Nana Janie took me here with my auntie. They are old. I am not sitting in the middle. At first they had glasses with drink and I asked for a taste. Then a hand came down with a big huge glass. It had red drink in it. I know the name of it, raspberry cordial. That's my poison now. The man with the big hand told me. It's lovely.

When we go upstairs to the dark place where Nana lives, there is a piano there and a table. Nana has to make things on one side and put them on the table in the middle. The piano is black. Everything is black. Butter with sugar is nice. You should try it. Uncle is somebody who lives with Nana. He looks like a priest, but he only rings the bells. Uncle plays the piano in a pub. I don't know why. He showed me how to play chopsticks, and another one – I think I think I smell a stink.

When Daddy comes he says, 'Very good, Joseph.'

Uncle says, 'You must get him an instrument, Tony.'

We are up one stairs, and up the next stairs there is a man with a white ball in his mouth. He has a bird in a cage. When we were there the man kept talking to me, and rolling the white ball around in his mouth. I wished he would move his face away so I could look at the bird.

They wouldn't let me stay to look at the bird. There is a bolt on the top of our door to stop me getting out. One time I put a small table to climb up on to open it. It was not high enough, so I put a brown chair on top of it, but it still was not high enough.

We have a new yellow table and yellow chairs in the kitchen. I was going to put a yellow chair on top of the brown chair but my mammy stopped me. She had a bamboo cane on the back of the door to show me if I was naughty.

Then they got me a dog. The dog was a puppy and it died with some disgusting thing in its basket. They said some B over the big wall in the yard must've poisoned it. I wished they never got it now.

Nana used to mind me. *Horsey horsey don't you stop.* Again! *Horsey horsey don't you stop.* Again! *Clap hands till Daddy comes home, with sweets in his pockets for Joseph alone.* Again! I don't know where she went. There is something wrong with me. I'm not happy.

One day Mammy took me to a street where there were women carrying sacks over their shoulders. That was washing for the laundry, she said. There was a house up some steps and a big door with a big stairs inside. A nun came and talked to my mammy and they sounded very bloody happy. In a minute the nun carried me up the stairs saying nice-sounding things, but I cried my loudest and kicked her shinbones as hard as I could.

The nun put me in a room with other children. There was a smell of milk with skin on it. I wanted to get sick. They threw pieces of bread for the children to catch. At first I thought it must be money the way they all ran to get it from the floor. That was because it was the last piece they were breaking and throwing.

Their back garden smelled horrible like burning when we went outside. I saw black snowflakes floating into the garden from the sky. I only went there one day.

Every night I hear things. I wonder why somebody screams far away. Children are shouting 'Picky Polly' outside. I know where they are, at the railings by the steps on the other side. Mammy came in and said that's what will happen to me if I pick my nose. Everyone will call me Picky Polly. That would be my new name. Do you see how bad that would be? So you better not pick your nose.

My throat was very sore and I was too hot. I had to stay in bed then Dr Stein came. The curtains were closed so the dark could not get out. Dr Stein gave me medicine. Daddy shouted at Mammy and tried to break the bamboo cane. But it wouldn't break so he threw it in the bin.

'Go back to bed, Joseph,' they said.

No wonder I am too tired with too many noises in the street. I'm afraid of the children who shout. But the big problem is there is always someone screaming. Sometimes it's far away. Then it comes nearer. Usually three screams. You have to listen carefully till you're sure they have stopped.

That's why I stay asleep after our afternoon nap in my new school. It's called High Babies and it's great. We have to fold our arms and rest our heads there for a nap. One other child sleeps long, but I sleep the longest – I looked over. One time Miss had to wait for my mammy to pick me up later and we were the last, and I was still asleep. Miss gave me sweeties. I am the best boy.

When I went home, Daddy had a present for me. It was called a flageolet. We sat together and took it out of its box. There was a little book too with songs, with special numbers and words. This is how to do it. Let's try this one. I know numbers, 1, 2, 3, 4. I can do it. But there was one hard bit, so my daddy moved my fingers for me. I was playing.

And Joseph would always remember that tune. And the song was 'Believe Me, If All Those Endearing Young Charms.'